Tales FROM SOHO

David Barry

This edition published in 2014 by
Acorn Books
www.acornbooks.co.uk

Acorn Books is an imprint of
Andrews UK Limited
www.andrewsuk.com

Contents

The Spieler	1
The Poet In Soho	13
Ronnie's Manor	19
Nude With No Name	26
Great War Poets	35
Soho Séance	46
Imagination	57
Sandwich Man	64
Down And Out	73
Home To Roost	80
Tricky Dickey	96
A Brief History Of Soho	107
Some Famous Soho Pubs	113
About The Author	117

Tales
FROM SOHO

The Spieler

Jess Bevan was a young man with high hopes. After studying drama for three years at one of London's most prestigious drama schools in the early-sixties, he walked the West End streets radiating a glow of optimism and felt he was going places. At first he attended dozens of auditions, and his aura of self-confidence, coupled by his good looks, should have secured him plenty of acting jobs. The trouble was, he failed to realise that his extreme self assurance stood in the way of directors employing him. They suspected his over-confidence was a mask concealing insecurity and an inability to be a team player, although this couldn't have been further from the truth. So, after a period of time, his self assurance began to diminish, and he soon tired of the company of other actors, aware that he had to lose some of his theatricality and become unaffected and more like a down-to-earth 'real' person. He was self-aware enough to recognise that perhaps being middle-class stood in his way of succeeding in a profession that was hurtling towards gritty drama and northern accents, kitchen sink and tough social realism. So he started to hang around in seedy pubs. And he loved Soho, with its striptease and clip joints, undercover porn shops, prostitution and illicit gambling dens.

One day, at one of Soho's less salubrious pubs, he asked around if anyone knew of any work he could do, and someone suggested that Spike Martindale (real name Eugene) was looking for someone to assist him and his wife in their subterranean spieler. Of course, although Jess was a middle class twenty-two-year-old from Carshalton Beeches in Surrey, whose reasonably well-heeled parents owned several gift shops, he was street-wise enough to know that a spieler was an illegal gambling den. In the mid-sixties there were no licensed betting shops, and bookies tended to operate illegally, bringing horse and dog racing a forbidden-fruit excitement to those punters unable to spend time at the races. Jess seized the opportunity of brushing with dodgy Soho characters as a way of gaining valuable experience and acquiring some street credibility, which he reasoned might help him in his future ambitions as an actor. His determination to become a successful actor hadn't been entirely extinguished by his twelve months' unemployment since leaving drama school; and seeing as the job involved illegal gaming, he thought it might make him some much needed money. With high expectations, he headed for a litter-strewn alley just off Brewer Street and found the unnamed club in the basement of a building beneath what he had been told was a "knocking shop". Whistling cheerfully, his optimism and excitement growing with the thrill of rubbing shoulders with the criminal classes, he descended the uneven stone steps to the basement and rapped loudly on the fading green door.

A woman answered, peroxide blonde, with a pink sweater pulled tight over pointed breasts, brassy and brazen, but with a sympathetically round and motherly face.

'I'm Jess,' he explained. 'I've come about the job.'

'Oh!' the woman exclaimed, as if there had been a mistake. 'A job, is it?'

'Yes, I was told... '

She interrupted him and offered her hand. 'I'm Vera, Spike's wife. It's not a job as such, but you should make some easy money, Jess.' She gave him a broad, warm smile. 'And I expect you're up for that.'

As she stood aside for him to enter the dingy hallway, he pointed to the dilapidated green door and whispered, 'What's that secret you're keeping?'

Vera closed the door quickly and threw him a startled expression. 'What d'you mean?'

'You know – like in the song.' He sang a line from it. 'There's an old piano and it's playing hot behind the green do-or.'

She looked relieved and blew out her bottom lip. 'Oh, yes. I quite like Frankie Vaughan. Now come with me and meet Spike.'

He followed her along the hall, past a hunting print on striped damp-stained wallpaper and through another door into a large bar area with an enormous green baize gaming table in the centre of the room, surrounded by odd chairs of all shapes, sizes and materials. He heard the clink of beer bottles as they came in front of the bar and stood before a man with a rugged face and dark greying hair. Vera introduced Jess to her husband who, instead of offering his hand to shake, plonked an open bottle of Blue Bass ale on the bar in front him and said, 'Good to meet you, son. Have a bottle of beer. Or is it too early for you to start on the sauce?'

Jess shook his head earnestly and turned it into a joke. 'No, I always have a beer at ten in the morning.'

'Good lad,' Spike said with a broad grin. 'As long as you don't make a habit of it.' He swigged from his own bottle of Bass, wiped his mouth on the back of his hand and asked Jess if he was happy to work on tips only.

Jess frowned deeply and asked Spike to explain, but it was Vera who answered. 'It means we sometimes get some punters in here who gamble big – and when I say big, I mean big. So all we want you to do is keep them supplied with booze, which ain't free, and once they hit a winning streak, believe me, a punter will hand you a pound note for a bottle of beer or a large Scotch and tell you to keep the change. For a large Scotch we would charge five bob, so you can easily make a tip of fifteen shillings. You only need two or three tips like that in a day and... '

She left the sentence unfinished, choosing to end it with a smile and palms-up gesture to indicate how easily money could be made.

'Sounds good to me,' Jess said. 'When can I start?'

Vera looked to her husband for guidance. 'We got that game starting tonight, Spike? I know Jim the Cat said he was loaded and fancied some action, but I don't know. I just don't know.'

Jess noticed how uncertain she seemed about their prospects, and he began to smell a little foreboding in the air.

'I think they'll be here,' Spike growled, frowning at his wife. 'It's game on for tonight.' The frown disappeared with a smile for Jess. 'So how you fixed for tonight? You up for it?'

'Yeah, sure,' Jess nodded. 'What time?'

'We're not expecting any punters until just after last orders, so if you get here about half-ten, it should give me time to explain about the prices of the drinks an' that. Oh, and something you ought to know: sometimes a poker game can last all night, until everybody's well knackered.'

Jess smiled and shrugged. 'I don't mind.'

All night illegal poker in Soho. Who was he to mind? After Carshalton Beeches, this was living on the edge.

Vera stared at her husband, almost as if she was trying to send him a telepathic message. 'You going to explain to him about the key to let himself in when we're not here?'

'Well, I'm not sure about that,' Spike mumbled.

'Well I am, Spike. Jess looks like a trustworthy lad.' Vera turned to face Jess. 'If we have a long session, there'll be dirty ashtrays to empty and wash, plus all the dirty glasses, and the shelves will need restocking with beer. We don't do draught beer, so you should be able to manage. Of course, we don't expect you to do this after a session, everyone'll be too exhausted. So if I give you a key to the club, you can let yourself in the next day around eight, tidy up, and maybe even be ready to serve, in case we get an early punter. You'll always have a float of about ten or twelve quid behind the bar, which you might need if an early punter wants a few sherbets.'

Spike fumbled under the bar and handed Jess a key. 'See you tonight then. And let's hope we get some extravagant punters.'

Jess thanked them, downed the rest of the Bass, and left hurriedly, taking with him an impression of magnified sleaze, the likes of which he had never encountered before. The walls of the basement club had been covered in a squalid maroon flock wallpaper that made the shabbiest Indian restaurants seem like palaces of gourmet gratification. Even the focus of the club, the reason for its existence, the dominant gambling table, had been pathetically neglected, with the green baize frayed and tatty with cigarette burns at the edges. And the place stank of stale beer, damp and cigarette smoke.

Jess loved it! It was just what he needed to coarsen the edges of his anyone-for-tennis image. But as he made his way towards Charing Cross Road, intending to browse for a while in Foyle's

Bookshop, he was disturbed by a niggling worry, a suspicion that he had been played for a sucker. It was the looks that had passed between husband and wife that aroused his suspicion. Why had Spike shown reluctance in giving Jess the key and clearing up the previous night's debris? Was Vera the one who was taking advantage of him, using him as an unsalaried servant, expected to arrive early, open the club and clear up the mess of the previous night. But she had mentioned the tips, and this, coupled with the exciting image of mixing with some of London's disreputable characters, gave Jess some grounds for feeling a little more optimistic about the job.

But that night, after he returned to the club for the first session and hung around with Vera and Spike, waiting for the punters to turn up, and sensed the despair and desperation of the married couple, he became aware of the extreme and pitiful defeat of the club. It had 'loser' stamped all over it.

Even Jim the Cat – whoever he was – had let them down. Vera prattled on about how the gambler was always up for it, and was a big spender, especially if he was winning, so something must be going on somewhere else in the manor. Something big: like the celebration of a villain being released after a stretch and being given the treatment.

But the evening was a washout and Jess left just before midnight without having served a single customer. Vera assured him that it sometimes happened, if there was something else going on in the manor that was important. Tomorrow would be different. Or as she put it, giving a poor imitation of Vivien Leigh: 'Tomorrow is another day'.

But tomorrow was no different, and when Jess arrived at half-eight and let himself into the club there were no dirty ashtrays to empty, no need to stock up on sold beer, no chores to undertake, only hours o f boredom stretching beyond closing time. Another washout.

On his third night, however, just after half-ten, a group of four men who looked like film extras from a Hollywood gangster B-movie barged in and said they were up for some 'action'. As they sat at the tatty green table, and Spike prepared to be a non-playing dealer, Jess put a spring in his step as he fetched the drinks for the motley crew of punters, observing the silver coins and paper money that was spread before them. This was more like it. Big spenders, and hopefully big tippers.

But when the gamblers paid for their first drinks, three of them gave him the exact money and only one of them told him to keep the change, which came to a mere shilling. When Spike noticed the disappointed look on his face, he gave him a reassuring wink and, as he returned to the bar, Vera, who was perched in front of it on the stool, whispered to him that he would do all right at the end of the game, especially if one of them cleaned up, which was what usually happened.

But it didn't quite work out that way. Around 2 a.m., with money changing hands back and forth between each gambler, and no one hitting it big, the game reached an anti-climax and the gamblers yawned and became bored and listless.

As for tips, Jess was left with some silver, which came to the grand total of six shillings, which he calculated wouldn't last very long. If he ate at the salad bar at the top floor of Lyons Corner House he could eat as much as he liked for five bob, but it would leave him with a measly shilling. He left despondently; shoulders hunched, but not before Vera explained that the next night, which was a Saturday, was bound to be good, bringing in a large and generous crowd. But Jess had had enough. It rankled when he worked out six shillings divided into three nights' work came to a lousy two bob a night. And his dissatisfaction kicked in with a vengeance, growing sourer by the minute as he emptied the ashtrays and wiped the beer-mucky bar at eight the following night. When he went behind the bar to replenish the beers, his eye was drawn to the ancient till, which he knew contained the float. He pressed hard on one of the digits and the till tray opened with a ping, and there in the slots was the float staring up temptingly: one five pound note, three ones, two ten shilling notes, and loads of half crowns and sundry silver coins.

Glancing over his shoulder, although he knew Vera and Spike never arrived much before half-nine, he pocketed the entire amount, the silver coins bulging in his pockets and jingling as he legged it out of the club as fast as he could, posting the door key back through the rusty letter box. He weaved his way past strip joints and clip joints, dodged down the alley near Raymond's Revue Bar, and sped towards the welcome illumination of Shaftesbury Avenue and the theatres, where he imagined his name in lights as he made a dash for Piccadilly Tube station, praying he wouldn't bump into Spike and Vera.

He tried not to imagine what would happen if he did? Would they guess what had happened and try to drag him into a back alley? He had heard rumours of stabbings and beatings in Soho, notorious as London's gangland and red-light district. There were even the occasional bombings in clubs, probably because owners refused to pay protection money. And then there were the razor merchants, the ones who striped you with a cutthroat if you owed them money or favours. Jess wondered if Spike was a razor man. He seemed quite easygoing, but if Vera felt cheated, Jess wouldn't put it past her to persuade Spike to do him in. Lady Macbeth out for revenge.

As he ran down the steps of Piccadilly station, he chased the Lady Macbeth image from his mind, knowing how unlucky it was to have thoughts about the Scottish play, especially when you've just committed a crime. But once he was on the Piccadilly Line heading for Hammersmith, he relaxed, and even chuckled to himself, knowing he would be able to afford the week's rent now on his dreary little bedsitter in a gloomy area sandwiched between Ravenscourt Park and Hammersmith.

But later on, when he thought about his theft of the float – and there could be no denying that it was stealing – he began to worry about the consequences. How could he walk the streets of Soho again or anywhere in the West End for that matter, without looking furtively over his shoulder? For several weeks he avoided going anywhere near the West End, but after a while time the healer erased his worries and he often forgot about his indiscretion. And even on the odd occasions when he did remember stealing the money, he convinced himself that he was justified in taking it, which after all belonged to him. He felt he had worked for it, and had been conned into believing generous punters would tip him lavishly every night.

By the late sixties, he didn't give the spieler another thought, even when he walked along Wardour Street, the hub of the film industry. He walked, almost strutted, with confidence, his head held high, because by 1969 Jess was a household name, starring in a situation comedy on television. Wherever he went, people recognised him and pestered him for an autograph. And far from shrinking and avoiding the intrusion into his privacy, he actually enjoyed the attention.

And once again Soho became one of his favourite areas of London. He was a member of several Soho clubs, one exclusively for actors. But Soho was very different from the Soho he had known in the early part of that decade. For a start, gambling laws had changed and there were now legalised bookmakers. And no more street walkers, prostitutes were now call girls who plied their trade by appointment. Homosexuality between consenting adults meant that there were now some openly gay pubs, and Soho had generally become a different, less threatening playground.

But Jess's dishonest past was about to catch up with him. Of course, the spieler went the anachronistic way of many of Soho's dens of iniquity, and by the late sixties

the premises had been thoroughly transformed and was a trendy Italian restaurant. So that threat had long passed into oblivion.

Jess's shock came in another area, not a million miles from Soho. Well into the third series of his successful sitcom, he bought himself a terraced house in Kentish Town, in a street of Edwardian houses, for many decades fallen into neglect but now gentrified and desirable.

Not long after he moved in Jess was leaving the house to go to his Soho actors' club one evening when he saw a neighbour two doors away, painting his front door. Before the man could turn round and see Jess leaving, Jess had stepped backwards indoors and slammed the door shut. He thought he had recognised his neighbour as Spike, the man he had cheated almost a decade ago. Heart beating a steady tattoo, Jess leaned with his back to the door as he considered his options. Clearly the old spieler proprietor lived only two houses away, so it was only a question of time until he recognised Jess. He would be bound to bump into him some time. And he was trapped. The street was a cul de sac. He had to pass Spike's house to get to the turning into the main road, and if the man happened to be looking out of his window...

Jess was suddenly very frightened. And he wanted to get to his actors' club and sink a few vodka tonics. Although his house had a small back garden, it backed onto someone else's garden, so the only way out of the house was through the front door. How on earth could he leave the house without being seen by his arch enemy? Because Jess's imagination kicked in, the actor in him exaggerated the situation, and Spike Martindale became a dangerous killer who would stop at nothing to exact his revenge.

Tiptoeing upstairs, without thinking how ludicrous he was being – for there was no way the spieler man could hear him – he went into his front bedroom and took a sidelong look out of his window. He saw Spike leaning back to admire his handiwork, and then a woman came out of the house and also admired the paintwork as she slid an affectionate arm round Spike's waist. But it wasn't Vera. This woman had boot-black hair and wore a colourful, hippy kaftan, and looked much younger than Spike. For a moment Jess wondered whether she was Spike's mistress and he had come round to help with the painting. But the couple's demeanour didn't strike Jess as two lovers with something to hide, the way they seemed relaxed and open, arms entwined, gazing onto the street with a territorial affection. After a while, the woman kissed Spike on the lips, and went indoors. Spike took another admiring look at his handiwork, then picked up his brush and paint pot and followed her into the house and shut the door.

Jess knew it was time to make his move. He imagined Spike and his girlfriend, mistress or partner, whatever their relationship was, would head for the kitchen, which would probably be in the rear of the house, like his own. He dashed downstairs and, without giving it another thought, proceeded down the three steps from his front door and onto the pavement. He hurried along the street, shoulders hunched, head turned slightly away from Spike's house and headed for Kentish Town station and the welcome darkness of his actors' club. But as he sat on the Northern Line between Kentish Town and Tottenham Court Road, he thought about his predicament and guessed there would soon come a time when he would have to confront Spike who would either recognise him, having seen him on television, or be told of his presence by one of the other street neighbours. The confrontation came sooner than he expected.

The following morning, feeling jaded after a night of excess alcohol, there came an assertive pounding on his metal door knocker. Bleary-eyed, with a throbbing head, he donned his white bathrobe, walked carefully downstairs as the knock was repeated – three loud tinny bangs – and threw open the front door. He remembered he had been expecting the delivery of a script for a TV drama production which he was keen to read. Imagine his surprise when he found himself staring at Spike and not the postman.

'Remember me?' the spieler proprietor demanded.

Jess blinked sleep from his eyes before replying. 'It's Spike, I do believe.'

Spike stared impassively at Jess, not a muscle moving in his face, slowly and deliberately examining the actor like a specimen. Jess wondered if it was going to erupt into a nasty and violent situation. *Not my face. I'm an actor. I'll sue if you damage my face* he heard himself saying but had the sense to remain silent.

As if weighing up the situation, Spike turned his head towards his own house before turning back to Jess and aiming a finger at him. 'There's something I want to ask you.'

'Yeah, sure, Spike,' Jess said in an excessively obliging tone. 'Go ahead and ask.'

'Can you let me have a signed photograph of yourself?'

Jess gazed at Spike with a numbness of expression, wondering if he had heard the man correctly.

'Only my girlfriend Delia has a young boy who loves your programme, and he'd love a signed photo – preferably from the series.'

'Of course, of course,' Jess replied effusively. 'What's the lad's name?'

'Daryl.'

'Hang on a second and I'll go and fetch one from my office'

As he ran up the flight of stairs to the small room on the first floor, Jess couldn't believe his luck. Guilt and shame terminated by a request for an autograph. This was true celebrity, fame being the spur.

He rummaged through his desk drawer and brought out a bundle of postcard-size publicity shots. He started to write on one, thought better of it, and pulled out a ten-by-eight instead.

When he got back downstairs and handed over the photograph, Spike stared at it, and mumbled, 'Thanks for that, Jess.'

'No problem.'

Jess waited for him to make a move, return to his own home, but there was a long pause as Spike deliberated, gradually clearing his throat before speaking.

'Funny we should end up living next-door-but-one to each other, ain't it?'

'Yes, I suppose... ' Jess started to say, but Spike interrupted him.

'Seeing as how nine years ago you legged it with our float.'

Jess felt himself blushing. 'Yes. I... I'm sorry... I... '

Spike raised a placatory hand. 'Don't worry, mate. I can't say as I blame you. I might have done the same thing in your position. I felt a bit guilty about the way Vera took advantage of you. We even had a row about it.'

'How is Vera?'

There was another long pause before Spike replied. 'She died of cancer in 1996.'

Jess became aware of the dryness in his throat, but it could have been dehydration from the previous night's boozing.

'I'm sorry to hear that,' he said.

Spike shrugged, looked momentarily sad and lost, then shook it off like a wet dog and grinned. 'But I'm with a lovely lady called Delia now, and she's got a little lad – Martin – ten-years-old, and we get on great guns.'

Jess nodded his appreciation. 'Good. Glad to hear it. And what do you do for a living now, Spike?'

'I'm a croupier at a London casino. So I tend to work nights quite a lot. But it gives me a lot of time to spend with young Martin. Hey! Tell you what: I ain't working this evening. What do you say we have a drink at the Alma at the end of the road?'

‘Well... I... ‘ Jess began to protest, and stopped as Spike aimed a stubby finger at him.

‘No objections now, Jess. Otherwise I might have to sell the story of the theft to the tabloids.’

Jess’s throat constricted, and what raced through his mind was the thought that – now Vera was dead – there was only Spike’s word against his. But then once it was in the papers the damage would be done; he’d be shown up as a petty thief, which in a way was worse than being found guilty of a major crime in his past.

Recovering from the threat, he chuckled, to show Spike how he thought it had been meant as a joke rather than a genuine word of warning. ‘What time do you suggest, Spike?’

The croupier laughed loudly. ‘Shall we make it an early doors? Say six o’clock?’

‘Sounds good to me,’ Jess agreed, still with some reluctance. Then told himself it was the least he could do to have a drink with a man he’d robbed and who was prepared to overlook the misdemeanour; which was how they came to drink together on a regular basis. And Jess occasionally wondered if the croupier might carry out his threat and provide the tabloids with the demeaning story of the stolen money if he, Jess, decided to sever their relationship. Not that he had any intention of doing so, because the two men became close friends, even though one had stolen from the other.

The Poet In Soho

As the beer-fuddled poet blinked the sleep from his eyes, he knew there was something he had to do, or something he had already done, but his mind was a raging blank. Raging blank! He made a mental note of the phrase before staggering into the bathroom, promising himself he would write it down before it was lost forever in his booze splattered brain cells, and wondered how many millions of the little grey devils he had slaughtered in last night's binge.

As soon as he had urinated copiously, he went into the hit-by-a-bomb kitchen, and found her note on the table. The note from his lovely love, his dearest treasure, and easier to love now that she had caught yesterday's late afternoon train for Swansea, leaving him alone which was how he wanted it to be. No fussing, arguing, or expectation of performing now, left in peace to be creative and write that poem that was buzzing in his head, tormenting him with words that he relished like liquorice sweets, chewy and sickly.

Scowling as he lit a cigarette, inhaling smoke deep into his lungs, he stared at the note as if it was a mysterious wartime code, though it was merely a briefly scrawled reminder, unsigned. 'Don't forget tonight's reading. And the suit from Moss Brothers.'

It started to come back to him, dripping into his brain like a leaky tap, cryptic clues of his impending poetry reading. Not just any old poetry reading. It was something significant, that much he remembered. A reading in front of – was it a royal personage or an important member of the cabinet, someone connected with the arts? What did it matter? He would give his best undying performance whether it was prince or pauper. But where was the venue? Was it Wigmore Hall or perhaps the self-important Guildhall in the City? His memory filtered slowly like coffee in the Swansea Kardomah, and he remembered they were sending a car for him at five-thirty, so the driver would have been given instructions. And he felt it was better not to know where they were going; that way he could surprise himself, indulge in a mystery trip and catch the venue unawares. He chuckled, coughed, and ash fell from his cigarette. Peering again at the note, he saw a writhing snake, a higgledy-piggledy underlining of the second sentence. Of course! She had emphasised the need for sartorial elegance. A dinner jacket needed to be rented for this truly important reading, for a performance which could lead to greater affluence and sustain his family and holy treasure for many months. Much as his mind was torpedoed with bombastic broadsides about bourgeois preening and prancing, he was nonetheless comforted by the delight of dressing up, which would remind him of his stage performances when a mere stripling at the Little Theatre in the ghastly, glorious town of his birth.

Later in the day – but not much later, as his surfacing had been way past noon – he sustained himself with two pints of bitter before staggering into the Moss Brothers gentleman's outfitters in Garrick Street, Covent Garden. The first member of staff to greet him was tall and stately, and he could imagine this dignified butler dishing out brandy sodas in some vast drawing room in a country house somewhere in the shires. And if this almost credible Jeeves registered alarm at his dishevelled appearance, it was but a brief flicker of the eyes, and the shop assistant soon resumed impassive dignity in dishing out the same restrained service on offer to every client. Soon the poet was kitted out in evening wear, admiring himself in a full-length mirror. No longer looking like an unmade bed, as some wag had once described him, but now cutting a dash in ballot box black and butterfly bow.

Careful to avoid temptation and the lure of the alehouse, he returned to his borrowed residence and soaked indulgently in a steaming hot bath, sucking boiled sweets and cigarettes. Proud of his almost two hours of abstinence, he dressed hurriedly at five-fifteen and glanced at his image in the mirror. Bow tie slightly skew-whiff but at least an improvement on his usual tangled appearance. Hair deliberately let loose in uncombed raffishness so as not to pander completely to the bureaucratic whim of the bourgeoisie.

His car, an impressive Austin Princess, arrived bang on the dot of half-five. The chauffeur saluted him smartly and opened the rear door for him. But, as poet and man of the people, in spite of the upper crust outfit, he refused the open door invitation and let himself into the front passenger seat. The chauffeur slid huffily into his driver's seat, and he could tell the man was a grovelling forelock puller, streets more snobbish than many of his passengers. So when he was gruffly informed they were heading for Wigmore Hall, he felt a strong desire to puncture the chauffeur's pompousness and instructed the man to head for a Soho pub instead. The man started to object but the poet waved it aside demonstratively, showing the fellow who was in charge.

They parked outside the York Minster in Dean Street, the pub everyone knew as 'The French', and without a backward glance the poet dashed inside. His intention was perhaps one pint and a whisky chaser, just to show the wretched driver how free he was from the constraints of convention; and then, having made his point, he would be a good poet and allow himself to be chauffeured on best behaviour to the venue. But there is many a slip, as they say. And the slip was the bibulous atmosphere of the pub, beckoning him away from duty, along with the other ragbag of artists, actors and writers, some of whom he knew, propping up the bar and imbibing as though their lives depended on how much booze they could slosh down their throats. Three pints and two whisky chasers later, his mellifluous voice soared in the blue fog of the bar as he belittled Wordsworth. His voice, cut with glass vowels from Oxford, still rose and fell in sing-song Welsh, and stories sprang from his lips with abandon, often punctuated by nicotine coughs. He was great company, and so was everyone in the bar. This was phase one of the evening. Next came the offer to his dearest friends, even ones he had only just met, of a lift to the next boozer, the Coach and Horses. Two of them took him up on the offer, while others walked the short distance round the corner. By now the driver was resigned to his fate, stiffly obedient, but comforted by the thought that he might get home early and still be paid the same rate..

An hour later the poet, in the company of an actor and a musician, tumbled out of the 'Coach', and the chauffeur-driven car was dismissed with a grandiloquent gesture. Every pub was now within weaving distance, and next on the agenda was the Dog and Duck in Bateman Street where, after their noisy entrance, the poet abandoned the bow tie in an ashtray and spent much time discussing Marx Brothers films. By now he was well into his cups, and after another hour of rambling conversations about Stravinsky and surrealism, he and his tipsy companions staggered to the Nellie Dean, where they consumed alcohol in vast quantities, drinking faster as their pub crawl degenerated into a race towards oblivion. Clinging to hazy parodies of sobriety, they then reeled into the Intrepid Fox, where they reached the penultimate phase of the night, becoming argumentative and contradictory. The final phase came a little bit further up Wardour Street at The George, where the poet fell over, tried to pick a fight with the musician over slurred disagreements about jazz and opera, before blundering into the Gents, where he bounced into the door, impaled his coat pocket on the handle, and ripped an ugly gash in it as he pulled himself free. A sudden agitation in his stomach was his last surviving memory of the evening.

Stirring the following day, a mouth like the ashes of the dead, and eyes that seemed to be glued together, he felt his bladder bursting, and groaned loudly as he dashed to the bathroom and made it just in time. The relief was unbelievably enjoyable, like sitting down and getting one's breath back after hill walking. When he returned, swaying, to the bedroom, and stood framed in the doorway clutching the doorknob for support, he spotted the sad bundle of his evening wear, discarded in a heap on the floor by the end of the bed. Head bent, he shuffled closer to the bundle, moved the jacket with his foot, and was horrified to see the vomit clinging to it like cereal in an unwashed bowl. He tried to recall the butt end of the night, vaguely remembering arguments and a fuzzy recollection of being thrown out of The George. Everything was hazy, like dream sequences in films. He gave up trying to stitch the pieces together and went back to bed where he slept for another two hours. When he awoke at well past two o'clock, his eyes focused on the degraded bundle of his rented dinner suit. He shivered from blood-lowering excess and finger-pointing accusations of his third-rate antics of the night before, then suddenly remembered the chauffeur and his appointment at the Wigmore Hall. He swung his legs out of bed and sat up, cupping his throbbing head in his hands. How could he have forgotten the poetry reading? And how could he now repair the blunder? There was no telephone in the basement flat so he resolved to go out and make his almost-needing-hospital-treatment excuses from a call box. But first there was the problem of the dinner jacket to sort out.

Still swaying and muddle-headed, he carried the Moss Brothers bundle into the small back garden. Rummaging in the garden shed, he found a spade, then buried the stinking bundle in a small patch of soft earth in the flower bed. Once he had patted the soil down with the back of the spade, and returned it to its shed, he went indoors to make himself a cup of tea and erased the tawdry crime from his brain.

Almost a week passed before the evening wear was noticed missing by Moss Brothers. A letter arrived, polite at first, wondering if the return of the suit had been overlooked. But the poet, busy broadcasting for the BBC, conveniently forgot about the reminder. A second letter arrived, now more assertive and demanding. This too was shoved into the part of the poet's brain reserved for trivialities, while he concentrated on creating a masterpiece of metaphors and imagery. But when the third letter arrived, this one more threatening in tone, and even hinting of legal action, he decided it was time to act. He dashed out and purchased brown paper and a ball of string. Then, returning to the scene of the crime, he went back to the garden and dug up the offending suit from its burial ground. Back in the kitchen he laid the sodden article carefully on two layers of brown paper. Lumps of clay now clung to the disgorged contents of his stomach and, holding his breath, he quickly folded the brown paper over the carcase of his evening wear, Never clever with his hands, except for wielding a pen, he struggled to tie the parcel and swore profusely. Eventually the misshapen object was tied with so much string it looked like an escapologist trying to fight his way out of a strait jacket, but at least it was secure. He stared at the slipshod parcel for a while, wondering what might mitigate the offence, and then it came to him. Of course! Why hadn't he thought of it? He was, after all, a regular broadcaster for the BBC and a poet about to have a five-thousand print run of his latest anthology. He would write a poem for the gentleman's outfitters which should appease the hardest heart.

He scribbled the poem, which took him no longer than five minutes, on a sheet of paper from a writing pad, slipped it into a matching envelope, attached it to the parcel and, feeling pleased with a job well done, rushed out to the post office. Once the parcel had been despatched, he jumped in a taxi and headed for the Star and Garter in Soho where he sat on a bar stool and regaled some of the regulars with amusing stories and filthy rhymes.

He never ever thought about the dinner jacket again. As far as he was concerned, the generosity of his poetic gift had wiped the slate clean.

When the parcel arrived two days later at the gentleman's outfitters in Garrick Street, staff stared at it suspiciously, and one of them suggested humorously that they ought to call out the army bomb disposal unit. The manager of the store was summonsed to review the situation as not one member of staff wanted to touch the errant package. The manager sniffed suspiciously, certain he could detect an unpleasant, earthy smell, then removed the envelope and slid out the note. His eyes bulged as he tried to comprehend its message. It read:

"Dear Brothers Moss,
Sorry for the loss.
Dylan Thomas"

Ronnie's Manor

Whenever we got nostalgic for Soho and its characters, the first name that cropped up would always be Ronnie Price, who vanished off the scene one day, and no one knows to this day what became of him.

Back in the late fifties, Soho was like a village. We all used to drink in the same watering holes: The Coach and Horses, the George, the French House, to name but a few. It was teeming with characters back then, and Ronnie Price was like an actor playing the part of a Soho reprobate. He must have been about thirty back then. He had medium length, dark brilliantined hair. Bit of a Tony Curtis look. Used to wear mohair suits. Short bloke, no more than about 5' 4" top whack. A real ducker and diver; constantly looking over his shoulder, like a bird hopping about in a park garden, one eye out for danger. Fingers in pies man. Always bordering on the dishonest, but nothing too lavish. Everyone knew him. And I think everyone liked him. At least, that was my impression. Even John Jolly, also known as Fingers, a bonebreaker by trade, let our Ronnie off the hook for a stunt he had the audacity to pull. Only someone of Ronnie's mentality would have chanced his arm and scammed a bonebreaker like Fingers. I think that's why people were drawn to Ronnie. He was naïve to the point of lunacy.

The incident I'm talking about was when our man of the world does some work as a bookie's runner. He was hanging about in Old Compton Street one day, keeping a lookout for the fuzz, when up comes Fingers. He wants to put a fifty quid bet on a thirty-three to one outsider. Ronnie looks at him like he's lost it, but you don't argue with a bonebreaker. He takes the bet, intending to go round to Tosher's to place it. But on his way to Tosher's he gets waylaid by one of the watering holes in our manor, and in he pops for a large Vera, which was his tipple. While he's imbibing, and listening to the cheerful banter of the natives, he overhears some discussion going on about the same horse race that Fingers has asked him to place a bet on. These punters reckon the favourite's going to romp it, and outsiders have got no chance. So Ronnie decides to stick the bet. He knew it was risky. But pocketing what amounted to almost two months wages back then, by not betting on a gee-gee that could end up in the knackers yard, was so tempting he decided to go with it. Trouble was, if it won he'd be right up shit creek, owing Fingers a sum that could buy you a reasonable gaff in Chingford.

Back in his scuzzy little Soho flat, Ronnie switches the radio on for the big race. By now he is shitting himself, and starting to have second thoughts. But it's too late. They're under orders, and they're off. So far so good. Dockers Yacht, which is the horse in question, hasn't been mentioned once. It seems to be a race between first and second favourite. Then Ronnie hears the news he's feared all along. Only two furlongs to go and Dockers Yacht is making good ground. I can imagine how Ronnie must have felt, cringing into his dilapidated old easy chair, shivering with fear. Then he hears Dockers Yacht romping home past the post. He is beside himself. And to add insult to injury, the shilling in the electricity meter runs out and he is plunged into a silence that signifies death and gloom and cold morgues. He sees himself laid out on a slab, and he panics, knowing Fingers will soon track him down.

Ronnie has no clear plan, but he knows he has to get out of the flat. Of course, he could have moved to another manor, left Soho and emigrated to Hammersmith or Chiswick. But our kid isn't thinking straight. He can no more leave Soho than Elvis can leave the US of A.

So by now he is quite literally ducking and diving around the manor. He thinks he sees Fingers at the top end of Greek Street and dives into a frothy coffee bar, an establishment he has always avoided like a dose. And to make matters worse, it is one of those gimmicky hovels where tourists and day trippers sit in coffins, surrounded by heaps of junk like the setting of a horror film.

So Ronnie is sitting in a coffin, and who walks in but Fingers. He spotted our lad and has come to find him. Fingers looks calm, and Ronnie wonders if he'll do him here, in front of all the customers. He starts babbling, pleading with Fingers, saying he'll do anything, even if he has to work for the next ten years to pay him back with interest. At first, Fingers hasn't a clue what he's on about. Then he twigs.

'You little arsehole,' he says. 'You stuck the bet.'

Ronnie can't speak. He is numb with terror, and the tacky décor of the coffee bar has taken on a truly sinister appearance. Suddenly, Fingers holds out the flat of his hand, and Ronnie cringes with fear.

'Give me back my fifty notes,' Fingers demands.

Ronnie is puzzled. The bonebreaker is demanding only fifty quid, which Ronnie still has in his pocket. As he hastily hands over the money, Fingers explains:

'There was a steward's enquiry after the race, and Dockers Yacht came nowhere. It was disqualified. So how come you didn't know that?'

Almost tearfully, Ronnie says: 'The shilling went in my meter, just after your horse went past the post.'

The bonebreaker laughs, because he is happy he still has his money. Then the laughter freezes on his face, and he leans forward and warns Ronnie that if ever he sticks a bet again, then he'll break every bone in his body. After Fingers has departed, Ronnie almost weeps at the injustice of it all. If it hadn't been for his poxy electricity running out, he could have pocketed the bull's eye and the bonebreaker would never have known. And this is when he discovers he has no money to pay for his frothy coffee. But that is the least of his worries, doing a runner from a tacky tourist trap. The kid legs it, and stays away from Greek Street for a while.

And that's what Ronnie was like. Always following his instinct, chasing a few bob here and there without raking in the shekels. A bit of a loser. But, like I said, a Soho character. And where would our manor have been without all these colourful creeps? But the wonderful thing about guys like Ronnie is their amazing ability to bounce back.

Not long after the betting incident, Ronnie gets the big idea. Way above his station. Talks big time, and fancies himself as a record producer, even though he knows not a crotchet from a hatchet. No matter. He has seen three chord herberts making much spondoolicks, and he is going to have some of that. But first he needs to find his gravy train. One day he jumps on a Piccadilly Line and heads for the wilds of Acton Town to do some dodgy deal with Jack the Nose who happens to live out in the sticks. Our kid is walking along the leafier lanes of west London when the heavens open up; a church hall happens to be conveniently near, so in he pops to shelter his mohair from the rain.

This is when he discovers three youngsters rehearsing their skiffle group. The lead singer, Ronnie clocks, may not be talented in the vocal department but he has fantastic looks. So it is now, he decides, that he must launch his new career. Money, success and fame beckon. And Ronnie has learnt enough about the record industry to know that echo chambers and recording techniques can make these little toe-rags sound reasonable. He's even taken to using phrases like 'augment the sound with strong backing', even though he hasn't a clue what it means.

He introduces himself to the youngsters, giving them the big I am. They are too simple to see through Ronnie, who can sometimes impress when it comes to the gab. And anyone west of Knightsbridge Ronnie regards as a country bumpkin. So it's not long before he has these three herberts eating out of his hand. Then comes the shrewd move. He singles out the good-looking lad, giving him some spiel about a recording test, and how he must journey up to Soho, which is now the hub of the music industry. The youngster, who I think was called Trevor Smith, is by now wetting himself with dreams of fame and fortune, and sees himself strumming and strutting in the cellar of the 2 i's coffee bar. If a Bermondsey cabin boy can become an overnight success, he thinks, then so can an Acton Town bakery assistant.

So it's not very long before Ronnie's showing him the sights of our village. And our kid soon susses that the naïve and star-struck youngster has been saving up to buy his fiancée a ring, which in those days was the only way to get a bird's drawers off, the engagement making it official and respectable, like.

So now Ronnie hits the lad with the agency joining fee, to cover the cost of photographs, publicity, etc., and the thirty quid engagement ring money soon finds its way into Ronnie's wallet. He reassures the lad that you have to speculate in this life, and he'll pretty soon be making a couple of thou. So far so good. Who knows: Ronnie just might have got his hair-brained scheme off the ground and got the lad a recording contract. But what no one knew, or even suspected, was that Ronnie's sexual proclivities were not as straightforward as he had led us to believe. He'd always had loads of girlfriends, but with the benefit of hindsight, I realise they were accessories. A smokescreen to hide his true leanings. And this is where it all goes horribly wrong for our kid. He gives Trevor, who is by now known as Ricky Cool, some more cock and bull about owning a big house in Harrow-on-the-Hill, and asks him back to his flat in Soho, using the lie about the house in Harrow to explain the scuzziness of his cramped pad, which in all honesty, he explains to the witless lad, is used merely as an office, or for getting his head down after a hard grind dashing from one recording studio to another.

As soon as they are tucked away in his sleazy dwelling, Ronnie, who is by now totally smitten with the lad, can't keep his feelings to himself any longer, and grabs the youngster's Hampton.

The lad is surprised and shocked, but he doesn't want to jeopardise his career in the music business, so at first he copes by merely pushing Ronnie's hand away.

'Oh, come on, Ricky,' pleads our kid. 'We'll just wank each other. That's all.'

The lad is disgusted and protests that he's not like that, but Ronnie won't take no for an answer and grabs him again. The youngster strikes out, and pretty soon Ronnie has a bloody nose. Dashing out of the flat, screaming blue murder and threatening to call the police, the youngster makes it down the four flights, but is stopped by the proprietor of the newsagent's on the ground floor, who is also Ronnie's landlord. And not wanting to lose a tenant, albeit a spasmodic payer, he manages to pacify the lad, and avert a nasty situation where the fuzz might have to be called, which, to a newsagent who deals in porn magazines from under his counter, is not ideal. Being an older bloke, he gives the lad some avuncular reassurance, and then sends him packing back to Acton Town, where he probably spent the rest of his days baking bread and apple turnovers.

As for Ronnie, he went to ground for four or five days. But word had got around about the scene at his flat, and when he resurfaced at one of his watering holes, the natives gave him some friendly banter along the lines of: 'It's OK, Ronnie, we'll just wank!'

You could see Ronnie hated it. And the more he hated it, the worse the banter flew at him. Maybe if he'd tolerated it for a few weeks, it might have blown over. But as the weeks went by, nobody noticed that Ronnie wasn't part of the scene anymore. Life's like that. Someone who's a pub regular might not come in for a while, and everyone thinks they're busy doing something else. And that's how it was with Ronnie. You'd often not see him at some of his favourite watering holes for weeks on end, either because he owed someone, or had some dodgy deals going on in another part of the manor. But then someone happened to talk to his landlord after a month had passed, and Ronnie had vanished. Cleared out his flat and disappeared. No one saw him leave. Just like no one remembers him arriving. He was just an element of our manor, weaving in and out of the streets like quicksilver. He had dozens of acquaintances but few friends. Which was why we knew very little about him. He was a man without a past, as if he had merely existed for the time he spent ducking and diving around our manor, like a character in a film that exists only for the length of their screen time.

I often used to wonder about the sense of shame that had driven him away. Was the disgrace of confronting his true sexuality worse than thinking his life was in danger when he thought he owed Fingers a small fortune? Or maybe he was just plain scared of going to jail for attempted homosexual rape. After all, homosexuality was illegal back then. Perhaps he thought there might be some backlash from the youngster's parents. Especially when it was discovered that he'd taken the lad's engagement ring savings. Whatever the reason, Ronnie ceased to exist.

I tried to imagine what became of him or where he went, but I gave up after a while. I just couldn't see him fitting in anywhere else. He was a Soho creation, and Soho needed characters like him. With Ronnie's hair-brained schemes and adventures, there was always plenty to keep the watering holes buzzing. Like the time he sold blue movies to Deaf Dave, which turned out to be a load of Keystone Cop films.

But that's another story.

Nude With No Name

Sandra Dorland had always been unconventional – perhaps even borderline eccentric – and lived each day as it came, never dwelling on the past or thinking about what the future would bring. She was excessively theatrical, and many of her friends and acquaintances described her as "camp". If you didn't know her, you could be forgiven for mistakenly thinking she was an actress.

And just to add to her own mystique and legend, she was of no fixed abode. Not that she was homeless or struggling – quite the opposite. She resided permanently in a small hotel in Fitzrovia. She had worked as a literary agent for many years, had never married, but had an affair with a world-renowned American author, whom she represented in the UK – an affair which lasted many years, although it was only ever when the author visited London, which he did several times a year for periods of two or three weeks, although he occasionally took her on weekend breaks to European cities. He also never married, and when he died he bequeathed his entire estate to her. She retired in her early-fifties, sold her small flat, and because she no longer had her occasional lover to visit her cosy South Kensington love-nest, she decided to break with convention and live a more bohemian, though hedonistically comfortable, lifestyle; one where she never again had to experience the drudge of domestic chores. Her small hotel had everything she needed, especially the minuscule bar and dining area, which she occasionally frequented; but more often than not she dallied in Soho with all her rather louche friends, many of whom were involved in the performing or visual arts. Of course, like many serious drinkers, there were those hangers-on, who pretended they were involved in artistic enterprises, but were mere boozers leaching off the artistic set. And, more often than not, they were readily accepted into the artistic faction, a group of outgoing people who were not usually judgemental, and were often too drunk to make a distinction between bogus artists and legitimate talents.

Because of the licensing laws in the seventies, pubs shut in the afternoons, and opened again for early-doors drinking at 5.30, so there were many small drinking clubs in Soho and London's West End. And most days, from about three o'clock onwards, Sandra propped up the bar of Sam's Place, a Members Only club above a tobacconist and newsagent's. But all that was about to change.

It happened one weekday afternoon in April in the mid-seventies. Sandra was as usual holding forth at Sam's Place, competing with artist Oliver Harding for the laurel crown of being the most outspoken or outrageous raconteur. On this occasion, Harding seemed to be winning by half a furlong as he had launched into a story about an orgy he had once attended, which was nowhere near as exciting as orgies were cracked up to be, totally underrated, and an experience he definitely had no intention of repeating. All of this tripping loudly off his tongue, hurriedly and breathlessly, so that he could enthral his listeners without fear of interruption.

Ken Smith, a walk-on in films and television, laughed loudly, hanging on Harding's every word, as if this were the Gospel According to St Matthew.

Perry Simpson, a choreographer of showgirl extravaganzas, listened intently, clearly searching for loopholes in Harding's story. He couldn't imagine this robust, overweight and bloated artist being invited to attend an orgy, unless one of the revellers wanted a quid pro quo painting, for Harding's pictures sold for a fair price.

The fifth person in the group was Margaret – no one knew her surname – and from odd snippets of conversation they dragged out of her, they thought she might have been a wig-maker for the theatre. She was the peripheral listener of their group, a role she was quite content to occupy, leaving others to provide the amusing anecdotes.

Harding was just about to reach the end of his story, desperately trying to think of an amusing pay-off, when Sandra's eagle-eye spotted three empty glasses, and she pounced during a brief pause in Harding's story to offer everyone a drink.

The artist put on his most affronted ruffled-feathers expression and boomed, 'You

interrupted my story, just as I was getting to the... ' he sniggered as he thought about what he was going to say, 'getting to the climax.'

'Oh, darling, as you yourself told us,' Sandra said, waving the objection grandiloquently aside, 'it wasn't nearly as interesting or as erotic as you were led to believe.'

He sighed deeply. 'Life is one cruel disappointment.'

After she had all their glasses refilled, she giggled. Harding asked her what was so funny and would she mind sharing it with the rest of the company.

'I'm just trying to picture you, darling, all that naked flesh wobbling. Stick to other vices. I don't think sex suits you. It suits some people, but not you, Ollie.'

'And what other vices would you suggest? Alcohol is my favourite, so I'm doing all right there. Or should I say here?' He toasted her with his favourite tipple, a large pink gin, a taste he had acquired during a spell in the Royal Navy.

'Have you tried drugs?' Ken Smith asked.

Harding flashed him a brief acknowledgment with an expression suggesting boredom. Been there. Done it. Didn't do anything for me. 'My last exhibition owes it's success to drug-fuelled perception,' he boasted.

'Oh, daaarling,' Sandra said, elongating a theatrical vowel. 'Next you'll be telling us that all those nudes you painted you could actually see inside their flesh.'

The artist stared at her with a mixture of animosity and affection. He loved her outspokenness, even though she had loudly criticised his nudes when she attended his latest exhibition, suggesting he found himself models with better bodies, a remark which hadn't gone down well with some of his subjects.

'Strange as it might seem, Sandra, I did get the feeling I could see them anatomically, seeing much more than pale insipid flesh.

But then, I seem to remember you likening their figures to slabs of meat on a butcher's slab.'

'A criticism you found flattering,' she countered.

Harding chuckled. He was talented, his paintings fetched ever increasing sums of money, so he rarely felt insulted or hurt by critical comments, although it mainly depended on whether he liked the critic, and in Sandra's case he did. She could get away with murder because he loved being teased, and suspected that deep down she respected his talent, and her banter was merely designed to bring him down to earth, and teach him not to fool himself into thinking he was the most important contemporary artist in the world.

Harding suddenly stopped chuckling, cutting it off as if it had been put on in the first place. He turned his attention to Perry Simpson, with the intention of putting the choreographer on the spot. 'And what about you, Perry? Your dancing girls have figures which most women want and all the men lust after. So what did you think of my painted nudes with their fulsome figures?'

'Well,' Simpson began thoughtfully, 'I like the way you apply the paint. I didn't really care if the subjects were fat and bloated. What mattered most was the stunning technique, the method you used to apply the paint, the style and flair of the paintings which shaped them into something unique. It's rather like some of Shakespeare's plays. The subject matter matters not. What's important is the writing itself. Like many great poems, it's the way of telling that counts, not the substance.'

Harding grinned. 'You know, Perry, I always thought you were a philistine but your estimation has shot up in my book.'

'Thanks for the back-handed compliment,' Simpson replied.

Four of the group sipped their drinks in unison, knowing it would soon be time to bring a new topic into the conversation. All except the timid Margaret, who was rarely sensitive to the adjustments of conversation.

'I still think you ought to paint Sandra,' she told Harding, beaming as if this was her own inspiration, and not a subject that had been hammered into the ground on countless occasions.

She felt eight eyes penetrating her as if she was a gatecrasher instead of a regular member of the group and her smile vanished.

Harding let his irritation show as he spluttered, a shower of pink gin issuing from his rubbery lips.

'Yes, yes, yes!' he boomed. 'We've been through all that.' He stared accusingly at Sandra. 'I could have painted her and turned her into a celebrity. Immortalised her. But she wouldn't have it.'

Sandra shrugged. 'I've told you so many times, darling, that I will never remove my clothes for you or anyone else. And that's the end of the matter.'

'Misguided loyalty to the past,' he boomed triumphantly.

This, Sandra realised, was a reference to her affair with her beloved author and remained silent.

Margaret, feeling she was to blame for the uncomfortable hiatus which followed Harding's remark, glanced at her watch nervously, polished off the wine in her glass, and said she had to see a client about some wigs. She scurried off while the remaining four carried on drinking and bombarding each other with opinions on diverse subjects, but predominantly the arts.

At five-thirty Sandra said she wanted to go back to her hotel to change, before meeting Oliver Harding for dinner at an Italian restaurant in Frith Street. She often walked the short distance to Fitzrovia, north along Wardour Street, across Oxford Street, followed by the short distance towards Fitzroy Square, but today she decided to jump in a taxi. Before returning to Soho to meet Ollie for dinner, she desired a long soak in the bath and wanted to read several chapters of one of her ex-lover's books – an obscure one which had been published only in the USA by a small Greenwich Village press long before he wrote his first bestseller.

When she arrived at her small hotel, she saw a man waiting in the reception area, seated in an upright chair next to an occasional table – an officious-looking middle-aged man in a grey three-piece suit. Her first instinct warned her that here was a man who was an emissary of distressing news, although she had no real reason to suppose he had any business with her. But Sandra always relied on her instincts, and there was something about the man which she found unnerving. Perhaps it was the way his enquiring eyes latched on to hers as she entered, as if he was searching for her identity, even though they were both strangers to each other. She felt like a criminal in a gangster film, about to be apprehended by a detective. Or even worse, she was an important witness in a trial and here was a professional killer come to eliminate her. Having lived so long in the world of books and fiction, she rationalised that she was being silly letting her imagination run rampant and dismissed her initial uneasiness, deciding the man was nothing more than a visiting businessman or a rep waiting for a business contact.

As she approached the reception desk, she thought she could feel the man's eyes on her back. Or was that her imagination being let off the lead again? She was keen to know if a parcel might have been delivered in the second post, a book by one of the authors she had once represented, but the receptionist was nowhere to be seen, so she thumped the bell loudly.

'Ah, Miss Dorland,' the receptionist said when she appeared from the office behind the counter. Then she looked across at the man and said, 'This is Miss Dorland, you're waiting for.' She looked back at Sandra and added, 'This gentleman is here to see you.'

Alarmed, Sandra spun round. 'Do I know you?' she demanded.

The man rose, straightened his tie, bent over and lifted a small attaché case from where it leaned against the chair, then said, 'My name is Mr Beckett, of Beckett, Gray and Garbles, Solicitors. Is there somewhere we can go to have a private conversation?'

Sandra felt hot and cold and wished she hadn't drunk so much at Sam's Place. She felt a strong desire to scream. What on earth was happening? She imagined her flimsy world was about to tumble. This was her world; surely it was not about to fall apart because of a visit from a total stranger. But the curious way the receptionist stared at her gave her some comfort. At least she could take this solicitor – whatever his business was – to a pub at the end of the street where he could divulge his business in secret.

In the pub, suspecting the solicitor's mission was not for her benefit, Sandra ordered a large brandy and let him pay for the drinks. Once they were seated in a quiet corner, he apologised for being the bearer of bad news before he tore her cosy world apart.

The shock waves as he spoke were like sharp icicles slicing into her. Her deceased lover, the world famous author, had an illegitimate daughter of around thirty-years- old, living in Los

Angeles. As his next of kin, of which there was not a shred of doubt, she had contested his will, and according to the solicitor was entitled to the money from his estate. Sandra was devastated, dropped her head in her hands and wept. It wasn't so much the money as the sense of betrayal on her lover's part. Why had he never told her about this other woman on the west coast of America, the mother of his child?

As she sobbed, the solicitor felt awkward. He offered sympathy and advised her to get herself legal representation, although he couldn't offer much hope of success in retaining the author's estate, but at least a solicitor might be able to help if it came down to the question of having to refund the money from the estate that Sandra had already lavishly blown.

Opening his case, he presented her with several official documents, then excused himself and left hurriedly, leaving her to read through the legal jargon and destruction of her world.

Dazed and dumbfounded, she returned to her hotel, where the receptionist stared at her, itching with curiosity, and obviously dying to ask if she was all right, the way she half opened her mouth to speak, but then changed her mind and strangled the question in her throat. Sandra ignored her, went up to her room, and had a long and tearful soak in the bath. After she had dressed, she glanced at her ex-lover's book on the bedside cabinet, deciding that as an early work it wasn't really worth reading and up to now she had been deluding herself about how good it was.

Once she felt sufficiently composed and able to handle the devastating news, she walked to Soho to meet Oliver Harding. As she hurried along Dean Street to where she planed to meet him at the 'French', she came to a momentous decision. She would go out with a bang not a whimper. Her brain reeled with clichés as she thought about throwing caution to the winds and burning her bridges. After several drinks in the pub, and while they were halfway through their starters at the Italian restaurant, she giggled and knew she was getting tipsy. When Oliver asked her what was so funny, she looked him straight in the eye and told him it was a woman's prerogative to change her mind – that's if he was still interested.

'That's a bit cryptic. Can you please be more transparent?' he said.

'If you want to paint me, I'm quite prepared to disrobe anytime you like.'

'What's brought this on?'

'Sudden impulse,' she lied.

Nobody knew why Sandra Dorland suddenly changed her mind about posing nude for Harding. Least of all, she had no clear idea herself why she did it, unless it was just a last gesture of bohemian behaviour, knowing she was going to have to carve out a new life for herself, and it was goodbye to Soho forever.

Two weeks after she sat for Harding, and the paint was almost dry on the canvas, she applied for a job with a small publisher in Leamington Spa and, because of her literary background, they offered her the position with a reasonable salary. She said her goodbyes to Soho and some of the people with whom she was reasonably close, and moved to Warwick, where she settled into a new and industrious life and became one of the leading lights in an amateur dramatic company. She cut herself off from her past life, expunging all memories of Soho as if it was a life that had been lived by another person, and never once travelled south to visit London.

Oliver Harding's star continued to rise in the next decade and his painting of Sandra Dorland was hung in an exhibition at the Royal Academy. He tried to contact her to let her know, but she seemed to have vanished completely, and he soon gave up trying. In spite of the change in the licensing laws, allowing drinkers the freedom to consume alcohol during the afternoon, he continued to remain a loyal member and customer of Sam's Place, even though most of the regulars he had known during the seventies had disappeared. He died of a heart attack during the late-eighties and Sandra Dorling never knew what became of the enormous nude painting the renowned British artist had painted of her. In the nineties it was exhibited in an Oliver Harding retrospective exhibition at the Hayward Gallery on London's South Bank. It was later sold in auction and purchased for 1.5 million to a private collector in the USA. The American died in 2008, having bequeathed the painting to a public gallery in New

York City, where it hangs to this day. In spite of much speculation by art critics and artists, no one has been able to identify the subject of the painting.

Sandra Dorland, the only person still alive and connected to those hedonistic Soho days, often speaks of her sitting for Oliver Harding. Unfortunately, she is ninety-eight years old, lives in an old people's home in Leamington Spa, and her ramblings are taken as evidence of senile dementia. So it is possible that soon her obscure fame will die with her and the true identity of the painting's subject will remain a mystery.

Great War Poets

Although I've been retired for a few years now, I hesitate to write about a strange event which happened over twenty-five years ago. I'm neither a religious nor a superstitious person, and I like to think the explanation for the death of my friend and client was nothing more than pure coincidence. But there may be others who interpret what I am about to reveal differently, and may well think of it as a supernatural happening. Well, that is up to them. All I can do is write about it truthfully and let others decide what to make of it.

I used to be an editor in a large publishing house based in Soho Square. My wife and I lived in a house in Highgate Village, and in 1981 both our children, a boy and a girl, were away at university. In April of that year I was drawn to Highgate Cemetery where Peter was buried. He had been dead for over eight weeks, but there was something bizarre and strangely haunting about his death. Admittedly he was murdered, brutally assaulted by a gang of drunken youths, a motiveless and pointless killing – but that wasn't strange in itself. No, it was something else which nagged away at my subconscious, as if his murder was in some way predestined.

Peter may not have been a close friend, but I was so haunted by his death that I kept returning again and again to the cemetery, and spent ages staring at the headstone, as if the answer was contained in the short epitaph. I was certain he, or someone, was trying to tell me something. And then I suddenly remembered a story he told me just the day before he was killed. It concerned an old lady in a shabby grey wig.

But first let me tell you something about Peter. He was far from garrulous, extremely difficult to get to know, and rarely spoke about himself. He was probably a little bit shy – certainly he was reserved – but he was intelligent and loyal. He was a talented young poet, which was how I became acquainted with him, when our company published volumes of his poetry.

He used to sit in Soho pubs, scribbling in tattered old exercise books, positively discouraging conversation with strangers by the concentrated frown he wore as he stared hard at his work. He would make a pint of bitter last a good forty-five minutes before buying a second pint, and he invariably got to the pub by noon, so he was assured of a seat before the pubs became crowded with the lunchtime trade. I would meet him briefly when the pubs reopened at five-thirty, and it was on one of these occasions he told me about his afternoon habit of writing poetry in pubs and consuming no more than two and a half pints of bitter between noon and two-thirty.

The day before the tragic murder he telephoned me at work. He was clearly excited about something and wanted to meet me at lunchtime. I asked if it could possibly wait until the following day as I was extremely busy and behind with my work. He sounded so disappointed with my negative response, I immediately changed my mind and arranged to meet him at the John Snow in Broadwick Street.

I've no idea what the pub is like now, but back then it was rather dingy. It was one of Peter's favourite pubs though, and I suspect he liked the history attached to it, the fact that it was named after the physician who identified the Broad Street (as it was then known) water pump as the source of the cholera outbreak in 1838.

I got to the pub at 12.30, just before the lunchtime rush started, and found Peter tucked in his usual corner, surrounded by his notebooks. But he wasn't buried in them deeply, shutting out the rest of the world, as I usually found him whenever we arranged to meet. His eyes lit up when he saw me. He was clearly excited about something and dying to share some good news. I bought us both a couple of pints and went and sat opposite him. There was no preliminary small talk. It was straight to the eager point.

'I've been dying to tell you,' he said. 'Ever since I got up this morning.'

'Is this to do with the feature they plan to write about you... ' I began, but he waved it aside impatiently and interrupted me.

'No, no. I've been meeting this old lady in a pub for several nights now.' Unsure of himself, he stopped speaking suddenly and frowned deeply.

'And?' I prompted.

'Look, this will sound crazy. I think maybe I'd better start at the top of the page.'

'It sounds as if this will become another poem.'

'It will. It will,' he agreed confidently. Then he took a deep breath and lunged into the story.

'Three nights ago I discovered this small seedy pub in the north east of Soho. I thought I knew most of the pubs in the district, but this one was a new one on me. Anyway, I'd been sat at my table for a couple of minutes when I noticed opposite me – at another table – an old lady in the most appalling wig. It was grey and lifeless and limp. It was the most pathetic attempt to cover up... her alopecia, I suppose. She was so obviously poor and I immediately felt sorry for her. When she thought no one was looking I saw her tip the dregs of someone else's beer that had been left, into her own glass. I was fascinated by this old lady and I kept staring at her. Once, she caught my eye and smiled.'

'And then, no doubt,' I said, 'she came and sat with you, gave you her life story, and cadged drinks from you.'

'No, no. It wasn't like that at all. You don't understand. She was beautiful. She was at peace with herself. Her face may have been lined and wrinkled with age, but her bone structure... I could see that as a young girl she must have been a beauty. In a way she still was. She just sat there quietly, enjoying her beer and reading a book. Which brings me to the most fascinating part.'

He paused dramatically, hungry for my appreciation of what seemed a rather dull story. I was dying to glance at my watch, but didn't dare for fear of upsetting him. I could tell it was going to be a long, involved story and I wondered how on earth I could grab something to eat without appearing rude.

'Go on,' was all I could manage by way of encouragement.

'It's the book she was reading. She was reading Rupert Brooke's poetry.'

He looked triumphant, having thrown this world shattering morsel of news at me. I couldn't help smiling.

'There must be more than that,' I said.

He picked up his beer, took a quick swallow, then placed the glass carefully on a beer mat. He returned my smile, and I remember thinking at the time that here was a new Peter. He was more confident, sure of himself, and quite self indulgent as he relived his story. And when he spoke, his voice had a slight tremor of excitement.

'There's much more than that. You were so wrong when you jumped to the conclusion that she came and sat next to me to pester me. It was the other way round. I felt myself drawn to her. I wanted to talk to her but felt too tongue-tied. Eventually, she looked up again from her Rupert Brooke and I found myself quoting aloud: "If I should die, think only this of me: That there's some corner of a foreign field That is for ever England". And as soon as I'd said it I felt foolish. But she gave me a beautiful smile and I felt a warm, helpless glow, as if a bond had been formed between us, and we were the only couple in that scruffy pub. And I felt... '

He broke off as a deep blush spread over his face. He was back to his usual shy self. When he picked up his pint, I noticed his hand shook. He put it down without taking a drink, determined to finish his story.

'The thing is,' he began cautiously, 'she must have been in her eighties, but I felt... I felt sexually aroused by her.'

I was shocked by this confession and it totally threw me. Unable to think of an appropriate response, I glanced towards the food counter and took the easy way out.

'You hungry?' I asked.

His eyes flashed with anger. 'Look! Let me finish. You don't understand. She was beautiful.'

'Yes, but her age compared to yours.'

'It didn't seem to matter. She was a young girl in the body of an old woman. It's hard to explain.'

He was right. It was hard to comprehend. Was Peter having an affair with an octogenarian? Was that what he was trying to tell me? A picture of two naked writhing bodies burst into my mind, one young and lily-white, the other grey and wrinkled and decaying, wrestling together liked the gnarled tentacles and roots of some deformed tree. I shivered involuntarily and hoped Peter hadn't noticed.

'What happened?' I asked him after a pause.

He shook his head sadly. 'Nothing happened.'

I'm not sure whether I was relieved or disappointed at this anticlimactic part of his tale. It was then I noticed I'd been digging a thumbnail into a corner of the plastic seat and had made a hole in it and some of the stuffing was coming out. I placed both hands on the table then raised my pint. But Peter had another shock to deliver.

'When I say nothing happened, I mean nothing happened our first night together. In fact we hardly spoke to each other, except for my sententious acknowledgement of the book she was reading.'

I had to admit, I was now over the initial shock, and couldn't have cared less about the food or dashing back to work. I was well and truly hooked.

'Perhaps that's why you were attracted to her,' I suggested. 'The poetry.'

'Yes, I suppose that was one very good reason. Anyway, I returned to the pub on the following night and there she was, sitting at the same table. And do you know what she was reading this time? The poetry of Siegfried Sassoon.'

He looked delighted with this revelation, as if it was the unravelling of a great mystery. I gave him a blank stare.

'Well,' he continued a little breathlessly now,' I wanted to speak to her – desperately. But I couldn't. I felt like... like a lover reduced to a helpless invertebrate, wanting to please her but feeling I might ruin things if I tried too hard. It was the next night I managed to pluck up enough courage – especially when I saw what she was reading this time. She was reading the poems of Wilfred Owen!'

I began to think this was the start of an obsessive madness, and he had stumbled upon some sort of soul-mate. Someone who shared the same obsession to the exclusion of all else.

'Don't you see?' he cried. 'Don't you see?'

So carried away was Peter, several people in the pub watched us with interest. I leaned forward and lowered my voice, hoping he would follow suit. 'I see the common denominator,' I said. 'They are all Great War poets.'

'Exactly,' he shouted, and smacked his hand on the table.

'Er – I think you'd better lower your voice. People are staring at us now.'

He looked to left and right, but seemed not to notice anyone, then straight back at me. He must have absorbed what I said because he spoke quietly, although his voice had lost none of its excitement, suppressed now with a kind of dog-panting urgency.

'I asked her why the Great War poets and she told me her life story. Her lover was killed in the Battle of Verdun on 22 February, 1916. They were both passionately fond of poetry. Their love was so great that... that she has mourned him ever since.'

'For sixty-five years?'

Peter nodded vehemently. 'Yes, she talks about him as if one day he's going to return. She remembers every detail of their brief time together as if there was nothing between then and now. No time or space between.' He frowned suddenly, puzzled and worried about something.

'What is it?' I asked him.

'It's only just struck me. That scruffy pub is called the Welsh Fusilier and that was her lover's regiment.'

'Well, there's nothing remarkable about that,' I said. 'I expect she deliberately sought out the pub for that very reason.'

Peter's eyes glazed over and there were deep lines of concentration on his forehead, like when he composed his poems. He shivered visibly, as if a gust of cold air had blown into the bar, although the door remained shut and the atmosphere was warm and bibulous.

'So much of a coincidence,' he muttered softly.

'What is?'

When he looked at me, I saw fear in his eyes, dark and introspective.

'After we'd had our conversation, and I heard her sad story, I got up and was about to leave when she said: "I'm glad we found each other." Not glad we *met* each other, but "glad we *found* each other".'

I laughed, partly out of nervousness and partly to try to get him to snap out of his weird mood into which he was sinking.

'I can see this will become an epic poem,' I joked.

He gave me a tolerant smile and then drifted off again. I found myself losing patience and began thinking about lunch again. At least I still had time to buy a sandwich and take it back to the office. I pushed my chair back from the table, preparing to leave.

'Are you seeing her tonight?' I asked.

He shook his head. 'No.' He seemed disappointed. 'I've got to meet that journalist who wants to interview me about my latest collection.'

'That's fantastic. I can see this latest book of yours will go for another printing in less than a year. And her magazine is widely read and admired.'

He nodded but his eyes were distant, and I could tell he was still thinking about the old woman. Just as I became enthusiastic about the magazine, so he became sullen and introverted, as if I was putting the wrong emphasis on the mood of our meeting. Well, to hell with you, I thought, and looked pointedly at my watch.

'I suppose you've got to get back to work,' he sighed.

'I must,' I said, immediately regretting the sharpness of my tone.

I caught a flickering and empty look before he lowered his eyes, grabbed his pint glass and emptied it. He must have known I could never truly understand whatever it was he felt for the old woman.

I stood up and offered him a weak, apologetic smile. He gave me a wistful smile in return and I could tell we would end our meeting politely, like two well-mannered strangers.

In the street outside, his behaviour was uncharacteristic. Usually he hated goodbyes, would give a cursory wave without looking in my direction, and stride off purposefully. But this time he stared at me for a long time, shifting uncomfortably from one foot to the other.

'She's waited all this time, you see,' he explained, like a little boy giving a teacher an excuse.

'For you?' I questioned.

He didn't, or couldn't, answer. His eyes had dissolved into the distance again, lost and confused.

'I expect you're looking forward to seeing her again tomorrow night.'

Obviously I had said the very thing he wanted to hear because he smiled at me. Suddenly everything was fine between us, as though all along he had been soliciting my approval. His eyes brightened and he gave me a tiny nod before turning and striding off along Broadwick Street. I watched him go, his old suede boots jerking clumsily at right angles, like an ungainly ballet dancer, and his shoulders hunched.

It was the last I saw of him. He was killed two nights later, on his way to meet the old lady at the Welsh Fusilier. A meeting that was so like a lover's tryst.

As I stood in Highgate Cemetery staring at his gravestone eight weeks after his death, thinking about his relationship with the strange old woman and his tragic murder, I heard the crunch of footsteps on gravel as someone walked by. It brought me back to reality and I decided it was time to move on and lay his ghost to rest. So I turned away, but before walking on I looked back over my shoulder and gave his grave a final regretful glance. That was when a wave of awareness rose inside me and I was engulfed in an ecstasy of discovery. Peter had been killed on 22 February, on exactly the same date as the old woman's lover in the Battle of Verdun, but sixty-five years later. The date flashed from the headstone like a neon sign. How had I missed it before this? And what did it mean? It was merely a coincidence, I protested to myself. And so what? We have plenty of those in the space of a year. And yet this discovery, coupled with what Peter told me about the old woman, titillated and teased, and I felt as I do when I wake up thirsty in the night to find I've only got one sip of water left in my bedside glass. In spite of my scepticism, I was intrigued enough not to dismiss the coincidence of the dates out of hand. My wife was away for the weekend, and on an impulse I decided to pay the Welsh Fusilier a visit. I looked up the address in the telephone directory, and later that same morning I walked as far as Archway, and when I spotted a black cab for hire, I hailed it – again acting impulsively – instead of making the much cheaper, and no doubt quicker, journey on the Northern Line.

I was excited at the prospect of meeting the old woman. I wanted to let her know about Peter, and share my discovery of the coincidence with her. And then the thought occurred to me that she wouldn't know about his death. He had only met her three times, and all she would know of their arrangement to meet on that fateful day was that he hadn't shown up. I was to be the bearer of bad news and I began to have doubts. Was I making a terrible mistake? Should I leave well alone?

It had started to drizzle. As I neared Soho and stared gloomily out of the taxi window I had half a mind to tell the driver to turn around and take me home. But now I felt committed, and I also felt I owed this to Peter. I knew he would want me to let this old woman know of his death, however difficult it was going to be.

(I recently tried to find the Welsh Fusilier but it no longer exists. It was located not far from Tottenham Court Road Tube station, so perhaps it had to be demolished to make way for Crossrail Link. Or perhaps it hadn't survived very long after my visit in 1981, which was far more likely.)

As the taxi pulled up outside I could see how dilapidated the pub was. I paid the driver and stepped out into the rain. It was only a few minutes after noon and I expected the pub to be far from busy. I knew the old lady would be easy to identify from Peter's description of her tatty wig, but I feared she might freak out as I told her about Peter's murder. It was not something I relished, but I had already decided that it had to be done.

Before entering, I looked up at the pub sign over the door, a painting of a young Welsh fusilier in an old-fashioned toy soldier uniform. He had little to do with the young poet who was killed in a lice and rat-infested trench at Verdun. Or, for that matter, a young poet who was kicked to death in a Soho street. Again I had doubts about what I was letting myself in for. But the rain was now pelting down and I didn't have a coat, so I braced myself and entered the pub.

There were only half a dozen customers in the pub, and they were all men. There was no old woman. I was partly relieved because I wouldn't have to face an emotional scene, and partly disappointed having come all this way for what would be an anti-climax. I sat on a stool at the bar and ordered a whisky and ginger ale. As I was served by a middle-aged man I guessed he might have been the pub's landlord and offered him a drink. He accepted a half of Guinness and thanked me.

I knew it was only a few minutes past noon, but I glanced at my watch from a force of habit. I didn't want to drink in this dreary hole longer than was necessary, so I decided I would give it an hour and then if she didn't show up I could forget about this pointless pilgrimage.

'I wonder if you can help me,' I said to the landlord when he finished pouring his half. 'I'm looking for someone who comes in here regularly.'

'I know most of the regulars,' he said, wiping the foam off his top lip. 'You're not with the force, are you?'

I shook my head. 'No, no. I'm just looking for this old lady who drinks here regularly. She has a badly-fitting wig.'

'Oh, yes. I've only been here just over a year now, but that old dear never missed a day. I used to set the clock by her. Used to come in at the same time every single night.'

I breathed a sigh of relief. Perhaps it wasn't a wasted journey after all. But then if she didn't come in during the day I wondered how I could kill time until the evening. I thought I could grab a bite to eat in a decent café, and as it was a Saturday I could catch a theatre matinee and return for the evening session.

'What time does this old lady usually come in at night?'

'She don't come in no more. Gawd knows how I'm going to set my clock now.' He followed this last statement with a glance at the pub clock and a chuckle.

'You mean she's stopped coming here?'

His laugh froze and he frowned worriedly. 'You ain't a relative or anything, are you?'

'No, just a vague acquaintance. Why?'

'Well, if you ask me. I think she's dead. She come in here regular as clockwork for Gawd knows how many years, then suddenly she don't come in no more. Stands to reason: she must've died.'

'When?' I almost snapped in my growing excitement.

His frown deepened as he sensed my urgency. 'When did she stop coming here, you mean?'

I nodded furiously.

'Let's see now. Must be about – mm – about eight weeks ago.'

I felt excited, jittery. 'Please, this is important. Could it have been February the twenty-second?'

He stared at me for a while before he spoke. 'Just a minute.' He turned away and consulted a calendar hanging on a hook on the door behind the bar, turning back the pages to February. 'Let's see now – delivery from the brewery was on Wednesday afternoon... and she was... ' He turned back to me. 'Yes, I can't really be sure but I think it was around that time she stopped coming here.'

I sat there stunned, staring into space, trying to order my thoughts into some sort of clear comprehension of the events leading up to Peter's death. I felt my lips move slowly, slowly shaping into a bizarre thought.

'He came back for her,' I mumbled. 'That must be it. He came back for her. And she knew. She waited for him all that time.'

'Are you all right, sir?' the landlord asked.

I downed my drink. 'Yes. Sorry, I'm fine.' I got off the stool and headed for the door, aware that the landlord and several customers watched me intently, puzzled by my strange behaviour. I turned at the door before exiting, knowing that as soon as I was in the street I would be the subject of the next conversation.

It had stopped raining and the sun was trying to make an appearance as I walked towards Tottenham Court Road Tube. I suddenly felt elated and I didn't know why. Maybe it was because I had become involved in something of a mystery, but at the same time aware there are no answers. And that can be a good thing sometimes. Sometimes it is better to invent answers.

I thought about Peter for a long time afterwards. Our company had decided to posthumously publish his complete works in one volume, and I just dared to wonder if the talent he had was inherited, a talent that was cut short sixty-five years ago in a terrible battle at Verdun.

Soho Séance

The night of February 3 1967 will stay with me for a long, long time, even though it happened more than thirty years ago and I was the last in our band to hear the news.

I'm a percussionist mainly, but had just done a session for a singer I guessed would be a one hit wonder, playing harmonica, an instrument which I learnt when I was at school, along with the recorder, and when I was a bit older I also became a competent pianist. Unlike other members of my band, I got offered loads of session work because I can read music, which was unusual in the Swinging Sixties music scene, although not unheard of. The session I had finished had gone on somewhat, with the producer tearing his hair out because the singer was a toe-rag and the studio was costing him money.

Like the Beatles, there were three guitarists in our band, and I made up the fourth member on drums. But unlike the Fab Four we'd only managed one chart hit, getting to number thirteen, which was where it became a chart stopper not topper, an unlucky number, meaning our next effort didn't even get in the top twenty, although it got to number two in Norway. Big deal!

Anyway, following the session at this studio in Dean Street, I managed to grab a pint before they rung the last bell in a pub in Poland Street. I walloped it down me in the ten minutes drinking-up time, and then headed for Carnaby Street and Josh's flat, which was above a boutique selling Mod gear. I knew he and the band would all be there 'cos we'd been rehearsing earlier that day, and when I went off to do the session, little knowing it would go on from late afternoon until closing time, they said they were going to Josh's place for a spliff, something to eat, out to the pub, then back to his pad for Scotch and Coke and a game of five card brag. When I got there – *instant relief* – there was plenty of whisky left. After the studio session I, unfortunately, was stone cold sober. I say 'unfortunately' because I guessed the three of them would be well into the talking bollocks stage by then, so I had a lot of catching up to do.

It was dark in Josh's flat, with a cloud of blue cigarette smoke diminishing the only light from an orange lava lamp, which is how I missed their condition. I poured myself a large one with only a dash of Coke and toasted Josh, who was sprawled out on one of his more bizarre collections of furniture, an OTT sofa, lime-green and hairy, looked like it might have been fashioned out of a psychedelic yak. But then Josh's flat was nothing if not wacky. 'I like living in lava land.' That was Josh all over, who was our bass guitarist. My eyes almost popped out on stalks when I noticed he was dressed like a cavalry officer. I expected inebriation but not being made to feel like I'd wandered into Madame Tussaud's.

Terry, our rhythm guitar and vocalist, was collapsed on a purple bean bag, wearing a dazed expression and, even worse, a bright red faux military uniform with gold epaulettes. Then I noticed our lead guitar, Den the Dude, was also got up in fancy dress, and garbed in an old Prussian-style uniform, complete with pointy helmet. He was sitting back in the candyfloss armchair with his legs draped over the arms.

I downed in one the tumbler of Scotch with a wee splash and poured myself another stiff one, sans the Coke this time. 'What in Christ's name you think you're doing?' I said 'I thought we agreed we wouldn't wear any stupid gear. Remember the last time we pegged ourselves up in fancy gear? Joe went ape? He wants us au-fucking-naturel. That's what he said. Au-fucking-naturel.'

Josh laughed. 'He wants us naked, you mean? Chance'd be a fine fucking thing.'

I ignored it and protested, 'We are denim, guys, not moddy-moddy two shoes. Come on, what were you thinking? Have you lost your fucking senses? Chucking our money away at Lord Kitchener's Valet? We have got another session at Holloway Road next Monday. You want Joe barging into the session again, waving that samurai sword at us? I was shit scared the last time that happened. I saw my life flash before me. And Joe promised us. He said our next disc's got a great chance to make it into the top ten if not *the* number one spot., and he'll put us out on tour supporting Heinz and the Tornados, but only if we have the right fucking image. We can *not* turn up at the session dressed like an army of freaks.'

'You finished?' Terry slurred. "Cos there ain't going to be no more sessions in Holloway Road.'

My temperature shot from hot to cold and back again like one of those hit the weight and ring the bell at the fun fair.

'What do you mean?' I asked as the warning clanged in my head.

'I don't think he knows,' Josh said to Terry. 'He ain't heard the news.'

I took another swig of Scotch. 'What news? What are you on about? I've been in the studio most of the day. Has Joe cancelled the session?'

Den sniggered. 'You could say that. Joe Meek has been cancelled. Permanently.'

I smacked my forehead with my palm and moaned loudly. 'Shit! Shit! Shit! What's one of you done to upset him? You know how paranoid he's becoming. He needs to be handled with kid gloves.'

'Whoa!' Josh said. 'Nothing to do with us, matey. It's not our fault Meek's gone and topped himself.'

I gaped stupidly at Josh. 'Topped himself? You mean he's committed suicide?'

'Yeah. He shot himself.'

Terry mimed holding a rifle and pulling the trigger. 'Yeah, after he shot his landlady. She probably came up to his flat to complain about something. Rent arrears or too much noise from his recordings. And he blasted her with Heinz's shotgun, then shot himself.'

'How d'you know all this?' I said.

Josh jerked a thumb towards his multi-coloured telephone. 'Phone's been going berserk all day. And it was on the news.'

I stared into my Scotch glass and felt like crying. Not that I would mourn the passing of Joe Meek, but he had given our band a good opportunity, and now it looked like we'd have to scratch around to find another deal.

'I have to admit, I'm not really surprised,' Terry said. 'If you ask me, he was turning into a raving lunatic.'

I sighed deeply and we were all silent, each one of us lost in our memories of the record producer. He'd been a brilliant engineer, there was no getting round that one. And some of his eccentric but genius ways of getting the sound he wanted went beyond what any other producer would have attempted. Like the time he used the unconventional method of recording the Honeycombs' 'Have I The Right?', with the group stamping on the stairs of his three floor studio and flat. It gave the record a distinctive sound like no other. And maybe without Joe's crazy idea of the stairs stamping the record might not have made it into the top ten, but thanks to his lunatic idea it actually made number one and sold more than two million copies world wide.

As if echoing my thoughts, Josh said, 'Yeah, you got to admit, Joe had loads of good ideas to create the sounds he wanted.' He blew his breath out forcefully, rumbling his lips. 'Even if he did have a screw loose. Like the time he threatened to smash me bass over me head.'

Den snorted loudly. 'Yeah, that was a close call. Man, that wild look in his eyes as he picked it up your guitar ready to swing. Still, you can't blame him. You played like a fart in a trance.'

'I was hungover, man.'

Den picked up his Scotch glass and waved it at Josh to emphasize his point. 'We all were, Josh. We were all still pissed, I seem to remember.'

'So why'd he pick on me?'

Terry giggled in a girlish way. 'I wouldn't feel upset about it. You were in good company. Remember that story we heard about Tom Jones coming all the way from South Wales for those sessions, and in one of them Joe goes berserk and waves a gun in his face?'

'You s'pose that's true?' Josh asked.

Terry shrugged. 'One thing's for sure. He never got any of Jones's records released. And you gotta ask yourself: how come

Jones shot to number one more than a year ago with 'It's Not Unusual' once he'd parted company with Joe?'

'He never reckoned the Beatles, neither,' Josh said. 'I bet his mistakes is what caused his insanity.'

Terry waved a disparaging hand at Josh. 'Nah. The thing about Joe Meek was his paranoia. It was always there, bubbling under the surface. He was a tragedy waiting to happen. But murdering his landlady like that. She didn't deserve to die. She was good to him in all those years and she put up with a great deal.'

The four of us were silent as our collective thoughts imagined the bloody scene in Joe Meek's studio. And then, suddenly, it was like a car hitting a brick wall. 'Jesus Christ,' I whispered, my voice filled with awesome realisation.

'What's wrong?' Josh asked.

'Today's date. February the third. It's the same date that Buddy Holly died in 1959.'

'Not to mention Richie Valens and the Big Bopper,' Terry slurred.

'Yeah but it was Buddy Holly who was Joe's hero. He worshipped him.'

Josh clicked his fingers as he recalled, 'And I remember him boasting about a séance he once held in 1957. Apparently he was warned Buddy Holly would die on February the third. But when that date came and went in fifty-eight, everyone thought it was bollocks. Until... '

'He died on that date in the following year,' I cut in. 'Bit spooky that, if you ask me.'

Den snorted again. 'Sorry, but I think it's a load of bollocks. Pure coincidence, man.'

'You've got to admit,' I persisted, 'he gets the right date in the séance. And that's one day out of three-hundred and sixty-five. That's too much of a coincidence.'

Josh waved a hand in my direction. 'Ray's right. The odds are too stacked up against it being a coincidence.'

Den laughed, made a howling noise, and clawed at his face as if he was being transformed into a werewolf. Josh scowled at him.

'Shut it, Den. Open your mind, man. Don't close it to anything that... that can't be explained by logic. What about Joe killing himself today of all days? The same date his hero Buddy goes down in that plane.'

Den swung his legs from the arm of the candy floss armchair and pulled himself up, swaying slightly. 'That's easy to explain,' he said as he staggered towards me. 'Geezer is so fucking deranged, maybe he's been thinking about the date all along. Becoming more and more obsessed.' He picked up the Scotch bottle and poured himself a generous measure. 'Apart from which, there was all that business about the frozen royalties from 'Telstar'. They reckon he plagiarised the tune from some French film. Imagine writing a mega hit like that and not getting a brass farthing. No wonder the geezer was off his rocker, and it was a question of time until he flipped completely. And now it's happened. So don't give me that – whoo-whoo-whoo – ghostly shit about dates and messages coming from beyond... ' An arm-waving demonstration and Den nearly lost his balance. He fell back into the safety of his garish armchair.

Josh jabbed his finger in Den's direction. 'You are a sceptical bastard.'

'Me?'

'Yes! You! You might be able to explain Joe killing himself the same date as Buddy Holly, but how do you explain Joe finding out the date at a séance over a year before Holly died. You fucking can't, can you?'

Den took refuge in a large drunken smirk which wound Josh up even more.

'Someone should wipe that stupid smile off your fucking face.'

'Oh, come on, you two,' Terry said. 'Leave it out. I know this bad news has affected us, but let's not start world war three.'

Eyes blazing, Josh looked at me and held his hands out in an appealing gesture. 'I'm not trying to start anything, Ray. But if that silly bastard over there could give me an explanation of how comes Joe Meek gets news of Buddy Holly's death date in 1957, instead of behaving like a half-arsed tosser he is... '

'I tell you what,' Den interrupted. 'Just to show you I ain't biased. We could have our own séance? See if anyone tries to contact us from beyond the grave.'

'You taking the piss?'

'No, honest. Hand on heart. Shit!'

Demonstrating his sincerity with his right hand, Den spilled Scotch down his Prussian officer's uniform. 'Now look what you made me do.'

Their animosity forgotten, Josh laughed. 'Serves you right.'

Terry suddenly launched himself from his beanbag, rolled over on to his stomach, stood up, then spun round to face us. 'Come on then. We having this séance or not?'

'You serious?' I said.

'Course I am, Ray. Let's do it while we are still in the land of the living.'

'Speak for yourself,' Josh said. 'I feel like an extra in *The Plague of the Zombies*.'

Josh looked like it as well. His face had turned to rubber and his glassy eyes were rolling in their sockets. But he still managed to stagger over to the small round pine table by the window, cleared it of KFC cartons which he took out to the kitchen.

'You got those letters of the alphabet we used in our last séance or we gonna have to write them out again?' Terry called after him.

'Yeah, they're here in the kitchen drawer.'

Josh returned moments later with a clean glass tumbler for our séance, and the letters of the alphabet which he spread out in a circle around the glass. Pretty soon the four of us were sitting round the table with a finger resting on the rim of the glass.

'Now what?' Den said.

Terry stared at him challengingly. 'Don't try an' pretend you ain't done this before, you moron.'

'Who you calling a moron, you moron? No, I ain't ever done a séance before.'

'How come we had a séance here last month and you wasn't in it?'

'Haven't a clue, mate. Must have been the night I spent with that little scrubber from Crystal Palace. I've never been to a séance before, I swear.'

'Lying git.'

'I swear on my grandmother's life.' Den, a grin on his face, took his hand from the tumbler and placed it over his heart.

'Your gran's probably six feet under. Now get your finger back on the glass.'

Den placed his index finger on the edge of the glass with an exaggerated display of restraint, and I suspected he was deliberately trying to show he had no intention of cheating by moving it. 'There we go. But aren't we supposed to turn the lights off?'

'We can see bugger all in here as it is,' I said. 'A lava lamp hardly counts as a source of light.'

Josh slammed his left hand on to the table. 'You can insult me, but leave me lava lamp out of it.'

'Shut up, you guys,' Terry admonished. 'Let's concentrate. Shall I do the honours and ask the spirits to contacts us?' Josh's head dropped forwards which Terry took to be an overstated nod. He lowered his voice from his usual high baritone to a spooky bass. 'Is there anyone there? Anyone from beyond who wishes to contact us?'

Den sniggered.

'Shut it, Den,' Terry growled, then resumed his invocation. 'Joe Meek, if you can hear us, tell us why you did it? Can you hear us Joe Meek?'

I caught Den's eye, spotted the cynicism, and gave him a warning shake of the head. A brief hiatus while we waited for a response from the beyond the grave. The glass beneath my finger trembled slightly. Was someone putting pressure on it? Josh, maybe? On the other hand, Terry was the one who had suggested the séance.

Terry's voice deepened, and I thought he might be parodying. 'Come in, Joe Meek. Are you there? Give us a sign, Joe.'

Almost imperceptibly, the glass wavered before moving slightly to my left. We all stared at it, wondering who was pushing it. I was sitting nearest the first letters in the alphabet and the glass slid smoothly in my direction. It nudged the letter A.

'Make a mental note of the letters as it moves,' Josh instructed.

The glass slid away from me across to the other side of the table towards letters at the other end of the alphabet. I wasn't applying any pressure, and as Josh and Terry were on the far side of the table, I didn't think they could pull the glass towards them.

Which left Den who was sitting on my left. He was the one who had ridiculed the idea of a séance, so maybe he was having a laugh at our expense.

'The letter U,' Terry whispered in an awed tone as the glass touched the letter. 'A and U so far.'

Slowly, slowly, the glass slid back across the table to Den's left. After a short oscillation, hovering uncertainly between letters D and H, it moved positively to F.

'A-U-F?' Josh questioned. 'That don't make sense. There's no such word starts like that.'

'Ssh!' Terry hissed. 'Let's see where it goes next.'

We all watched as it went across the other side to W, then to I, followed by E.

'I'll never remember these letters,' Den said. 'It's not a proper word.'

As the glass slid to the letter D, Josh chuckled knowingly. 'I think it is. And if I'm right A-U-F was one word and this is the second word.'

The glass moved quicker now, as if whoever was pushing it was getting impatient.

'Oh, bloody hellfire,' Den moaned. 'I can't remember all these letters.'

As the glass finished off the second word, Josh said, 'No wonder it took us a while to recognise it. It's German. *Auf Wiedersehen.*'

'Who is sending us this message?' Terry intoned in an other-worldly voice. 'Tell us who you are.'

The glass shot across to the letter J, and I guessed what was coming next. Sure enough, after a hesitant move, hovering uncertainly between letters, the glass finished off the name. JOE.

I knew then this was a hoax. It was obvious by the way an interval had been left after spelling the first letter of his name in order to build the suspense.

'Fuck me!' Den gasped. 'What does *Auf Wiedersehen* mean anyway? Goodbye, isn't it?'

Josh stared at him, eyes like the barroom baddie in a B-western. 'You know fuckin' well what it means. Don't bullshit a bullshitter.'

'What are you on about?'

Josh slammed an angry fist onto the table. 'I'm on about you, you cheating bastard. Remember that talk we had months ago about Joe?'

'How am I supposed to remember... ' Den began, but was stopped by the séance tumbler smashing into the wall where Josh had suddenly thrown it.

Terry and I froze, wondering what would happen next. Maybe, I thought, the smashed glass would be enough to quell Josh's temper, and when I saw him point an accusing finger at Den I guessed the worst was over. But I was wrong.

'You don't remember, you lying wanker, the conversation we had about Joe's work he did as a recording engineer with singers like Anne Shelton. You've fucking forgotten, have you, how you asked if he'd ever done any Vera Lynn and you suddenly burst into song? *Auf wiedersehen, we'll meet again.* You lying, dirty, rotten, cheating bastard.'

And that might have been that. It might have blown over at that point had Den not laughed and said, 'Don't get your knickers in a twist, man. I thought you might like Joe's little message. He meant to say 'so long, suckers'.'

The rim of the table hit me in the stomach as Josh jumped up, taking the table with him. He barged between Terry and the overturned table and grabbed a cowering Den by the throat, drawing back his fist ready to pound him to a pulp.

'Josh!' Terry screamed. 'Hey, man! Calm down!'

I leapt up and grabbed Josh's elbow to stop him slamming Den, but couldn't make contact and I heard the dull smack as fist met face. Den yelled, 'Ah! You crazy bastard.'

By now, Terry was restraining Josh with both arms wrapped around him. Blood streamed from our lead guitarist's nose. The scene was surreal, like we were overactive zombies in a lava-lit aquarium. At the same time, as Josh apologised to Den—'Hey, man! I'm sorry, I'm sorry' – I began to find the commotion amusing, as I observed the bizarre scene of the three long-haired musicians weaving and swaying in their military costumes. I can remember collapsing with laughter, doubling-up while Den admonished me and complaining that his nose must be broken. It wasn't. When the bleeding stopped, and after close examination, he admitted there was no lasting damage. Then came recriminations, Josh weeping with guilt, cuddling Den and swearing undying love. More drinks were poured. Another joint was rolled. And then, lying back in a stupefied state we talked softly about Joe Meek and his legacy. The night passed in a haze, and I don't remember much about the early hours as I half dozed, resurfacing every so often to smoke and drink.

What happened after that was inevitable. With Joe Meek dead, and unable to find another record producer our band eventually split up. We all went our separate ways

and I never discovered what became of Terry, Den and Josh. As the years passed, and the pages flew off the calendar, I thought I might hear of at least one of them playing in another group somewhere. But I never heard a dickey-bird, so I guessed they must have done the same as me – settled down, got a proper job and got married.

It was like my rock 'n' roll years happened to someone else in another life. And if I'm honest a band with a cruddy name like ours would have become nothing but a joke as the years wore on. Marvin and the Movers. I ask you.

Marvin and the Movers. R.I.P.

Imagination

Erica Smith got off the Central Line at Oxford Circus, walked past the London Palladium, and turned left into Great Marlborough Street. The building, she'd been told, was not far beyond the Magistrates' Court. She tried to picture the premises, wondering in her naïve mind's eye whether it might be like a film setting, the disturbing ones with dream sequences full of strange angles and shadows.

To her surprise, the building was nothing how she imagined it. It was modern, glass and chrome, with a huge advertisement in the window for what appeared to be something obscure and incomprehensible, so she rejected it with a clean wipe from her mind. It was like that with anything she didn't understand. She was never stimulated by questions and conundrums and was unencumbered by an enquiring mind.

She walked past the gaping glass and found the entrance just the other side of the baffling display, and stood small before a looming black door. A lump like sickly dough rose in her throat and she suddenly felt nervous, twitchy. What if she failed the test? It was only a game of pretend she told herself, using a soft silky voice to turn them on. And the man – what was his name? – Terry, that was it. Terry had told her she had to use the dirtiest imagination she had, the dirtier the better, which was what they liked.

Stomach fluttering, breath tremulous as she exhaled, she rang the bell, expecting a voice to speak to her. Instead, she heard a buzz and click. She pushed open the door and entered the darkness of the hall. Nothing on the ground floor, just a staircase leading up to a door marked 'Toilet' on the first floor landing.

Wooden groans came from beneath the thin carpet as she climbed the stairs, breathing heavily, discomfited by the thoughts of giving a convincing performance. As she rounded the top of the stairs, she saw the other door with a bold red name on a long grey plastic strip. She had arrived at Intercourse Enterprises.

She tapped the door lightly and entered, thinking she might find something seedy and sordid on the other side, although she hadn't a clue what that might be. She was surprised to discover an office, pretty ordinary and much like other offices, with two sofas, a receptionist's desk, and a water cooler. The blonde receptionist flashed her a smile and introduced herself.

'Hello. I'm Tina. You must be Erica.'

'Hello,' she replied, her voice husky with nerves. She hoped it made her sound sexy instead of scared witless. 'I've come for the telephone test.'

The receptionist giggled and nodded knowingly, as if they already shared secrets together. Another door opened near her desk and two men entered. One of them was dark and swarthy, dressed in a suit of shiny blue, with a slim tie and button-down collar. The other wore black jeans and a brown leather jacket.

'I'm Terry,' said the man in the suit. 'And this is Colin. We'll show you around, Erica, so you can see how it all works. The first phone call will be from a real punter and we'll be monitoring the call. This'll be your audition and we'll be listening in to see how you do. Sometimes it's best to introduce yourself and go for a slow build up before starting on the real dirty talk.'

The man in leather laughed and exchanged a knowing look with his business partner before he turned to her and said, 'That way the phone call lasts longer and we all make more money, because you get twenty per cent of all your calls, and some of the punters can run up a bill of ten quid in just ten minutes.'

'Think you can do that?' Terry said, staring at her intensely.

She nodded and swallowed, already feeling dry and thirsty. 'I'll give it a go,' she replied, hoping she sounded reasonably enthusiastic.

'Good girl. If you'd like to follow us.'

As Terry opened the door, an enormous middle-aged woman waddled through. 'Where you off to, Sheila?'

'Need the loo, sweetheart.'

Terry laughed. 'Well, don't be long. You've got a load of horny punters clamouring for your services.'

Erica watched open-mouthed as the obese woman shuffled across the office. Then she followed Terry through the door into another room, followed by Colin. The room had a long desk, L-shaped and built into the wall, with many computers and telephones stacked neatly along it, their monitors glistening like rows of eyes peering at Erica like aliens.

Terry sniggered. 'The look on your face just then. When you saw how fat Sheila is.'

Erica felt sudden heat from a blush. 'No... I... ' she started to protest.

'Sheila's one of our best employees,' Colin explained. 'It's all in the voice performance, you see. Because she's awesome on the phone, men imagine she's sexy and stunning. Little do they know.' He laughed as a thought struck him. 'Worth her weight in gold, she is.'

Terry rolled his eyes, and Erica got the impression that the two men's banter was always the same, feeding off each other like a double-act. At least it made her feel at ease. First impression of Terry worried her, the way he looked forbiddingly like a gangster in a film, but as soon as he smiled she felt reassured. Although the thoughts of what lay ahead with her test was like a grinding in her chest. She tried to imagine her own voice talking to her about sex, but the voice ground to a finish before it got going.

'So! Shall we give it a crack?' Terry said, pointing to another door in the room where the desk ended. Through there are six rooms – you'll be in Number Four for your test. We'll divert one of the calls to that room and then we can hear what you're made of.'

'Something you ought to know,' Colin added. 'We call them rooms but really they're just cubicles with doors, and the sound-proofing's not perfect, so try not to yell "yes, yes, yes" when a geezer's on the short strokes. Always keep the voice low and sexy. And we would sooner you use your imagination when you speak to the bloke. Really go for it. But just in case you dry up, there's a script in front of you with a few phrases you can use. But use the script as a last resort. It's really an aide-memoire.'

Erica looked at him blankly. 'Sorry?'

'An aid to the memory. Right, Terry, d'you want to take Erica through to Number Four, and I'll divert the next call to her.'

Terry ushered her through to the next room and showed her into one of the small cubicles, which was nothing more than a claustrophobic cell with a blank wall, a desk and a telephone and two pages of script. Terry wished her luck, told her to imagine the meagre room was her bedroom and she was dressed in erotic clothes. Then he shut the door and she was left staring tensely at the telephone. She had never really been good on the telephone, even talking to her friends. And staring at the silent telephone in the coffin of the room, made it even more of an instrument of pain. She was reminded of those agonizing days at school when she was forced to read something out loud, and they all laughed. She had enough self-awareness to recognise the fault, sensing her voice lacked the light and shade of emotion, yet she was still incapable of attuning it to her own ear. .

Suddenly, the jarring buzz of the telephone made her jump. Instead of letting it ring for a bit to give herself time to think, she snatched it up hurriedly and spoke in a nervous monotone without a space.

'Hello my name is Erica how can I help you?'

There was brief pause at the other end, perhaps the caller thought he had dialled a wrong number.

In the computer room, Terry looked at Colin, raised his eyebrows and shook his head. As they listened intently, they began snorting and giggling as they heard her reading badly from the script. But when they discovered three minutes had gone by, and the caller was still on the line listening to her pathetic attempts at dirty talk, and then it ran to four minutes, they exchanged puzzled looks, wondering if this was some sort of anti-erotic conversation that might turn some men on. The call went to just over five minutes and they thought she might have hit on a novel way of arousal. They didn't really care one way or the other. As long as she could average five minute conversations, she would make them money.

***

My wife and I split up six months ago. I was feeling lonely one night, turned a page of the free newspaper I'd picked up at the station, and happened to see the adverts for erotic phone calls. They were premium line numbers, and I knew it would add a lot to my phone bill, but I was in need of an erotic conversation, something to help me relax and forget about my loneliness and frustration for a little while. So I dialled the number. It rang once before she answered. After the preliminaries she began her act. It was not good. In fact, it was terrible. And then I felt sorry for her. She was clearly someone who hadn't a clue how to go about holding any sort of conversation, let alone an erotic one. And I suspected she was probably reading from a script. I faked interest, listened politely for five minutes, then groaned.

'How was it?' she asked.

'Great,' I lied, not wanting to hurt her feelings

***

That evening in the Shakespeare's Head, Terry stared into his empty glass, frowning as he tried to work out what had happened with that first phone call.

Colin came over to their table with fresh pints. 'I still don't get it,' he said, carrying on the conversation from before he went to replenish their drinks. 'That first phone call, the guy was turned on by it. Turned on! What's happening, Terry?'

Terry shrugged. 'Ain't got a clue, mate. Maybe he thought she would get better instead of worse.'

'That can't have been it. We heard him groan. She did the job for him.'

'I must admit it was very odd. Her dirty talk wouldn't have aroused someone who's been marooned on a desert island for twenty years. They'd have been glad of their own company.'

Colin sighed hugely, blowing out his lips. 'We should never have given her another three attempts. We should have got rid of her after the second call. That lasted less than a minute. The poor bastard couldn't take that expressionless voice and told her to fuck off. We should have got rid of her then.'

Terry laughed in spite of the loss of custom which he knew they'd never get back. 'Well, let's face it, we thought she must have had something going for her after the first one. Though just what that was is anybody's guess.'

Colin took a large swig of beer then banged his glass on to the table. 'One thing's for sure. I'm glad we kicked her into touch. I think we might have learnt a few lessons from her though.'

Terry tilted his head and looked at his partner dubiously. 'Oh yeah? And what have we learnt?'

'Don't judge by appearances for a start. She was quite attractive, but give me Sheila any day. Built like a brickie but the punters imagine she's the most seductive thing on the planet. Voice like an angel of eroticism, you see.'

'It's not just the voice, Colin. It's how fired up her imagination is once she gets going. And that's what it's all about. Imagination. Imagination's what made Mozart write operas, and how Van Goth painted those sunflowers they way he did, and the way Agatha Christie invented all them mysteries.'

Colin spluttered into his drink. 'Don't get all philosophical on me. All the phone calls require is dirty sex talk. That's all it is. Dirty talk.'

Terry jabbed an index finger on the table to emphasise his point. 'Ah, but for that you need imagination. And what we've been through this afternoon proves it. She never had no imagination. End of story.'

***

As it was a reasonably warm day, she walked through Soho and found a coffee and sandwich shop with chairs outside on the pavement. She bought herself a large cappuccino and sat gazing listlessly at the passers-by. Her brain had been numbed by her experience of trying to arouse strangers on the telephone. She knew she wasn't cut out for it. It was embarrassing having to delve into thoughts that were private and then having to reveal them. And as for that script... she could feel herself blushing as she stirred her sweetened coffee and thought about it. But the worst part of it was the dismissive way that Terry had brushed her off as if she was an irritating insect, telling her she had as much imagination as a lump of lard. She felt like crying then, but managed to control it. She didn't want to give those men the satisfaction., so she pouted and shrugged instead as she crossed the reception, and felt the receptionist's eyes following her as she dwindled away, feeling smaller with every step she took. As soon as she reached the street, she took a deep breath, and the smell of taxi diesel felt comforting and real after the neutral office smell.

Anyway, she told herself as she sipped her coffee, it had nothing to do with imagination. It was talking dirty, a completely different thing. Of course she had imagination. She looked across the street at a telephone box where a man was talking on the telephone, which caused her to wonder why people still used phone boxes when everyone had mobiles these days. He seemed to have been talking for a long time. Not just a quick call. Her gaze went up from the telephone box to the high building opposite and she imagined there was a man there with a gun trained on the man in the phone box, and he didn't dare leave otherwise he'd be shot, just like that film with Colin Farrell. But then she saw the man leaving the box unscathed and walking down the street close to where she sat, so that signalled the end of the drama in her head.

Moments later she watched a young woman in a red miniskirt pass the coffee bar, wearing high, high heels and showing a lot of cleavage. Her eyes followed the woman down the street to the busier corner, where she expected to see a limousine open its windows with Richard Gere offering her a lift. But when the woman rounded the corner, the dream disappeared with her.

Erica suddenly felt at ease and breathed in contentedly, smelling the different café smells of fresh bread, coffee and garlic. She would worry about the search for another job tomorrow. Today she would walk to Tottenham Court Road Tube station and catch the Central Line back to Stratford and go and see a film. She liked films, all kinds of films. She wasn't fussy. She could get lost in all those different worlds.

And who was he to tell her she had no imagination? Films gave her all the imagination she needed.

Sandwich Man

The hard leather straps of the sandwich board cut into Bill Flintlock's shoulders as he crossed the busy thoroughfare. His legs ached, and he had to summon up enough energy to leap out of the path of the horses pulling an omnibus. He cursed the beasts as he reached the safety of the pavement on the opposite side of Shaftsbury Avenue. If there was one thing he loathed, it was horses. Nasty, unpredictable creatures. He had been bitten by one when he was a young lad. Finding half a carrot in the gutter, he had innocently offered it to a rather mild-looking, raggedy pony. Not only did the brute crunch the carrot, it also crunched his fingers. How was he supposed to know he should have offered the carrot on the flat of his hand? No one had ever told him. It was all very well explaining after the event, but by then the damage was done.

Getting his breath back, he stood for a moment in front of the new Lyric Theatre and surveyed the congestion on the Avenue, thick with horses, cabs, brewery drays, coaches and omnibuses. The new underground railways branching out across the metropolis was a comforting thought to a horse-hater like Bill Flintlock, who couldn't wait for progress to sound the death knell for the equine brutes.

He scratched his unkempt, grizzled beard and licked his lips. Although he was only thirty-two-years-old, the ravages of a hard, poverty-stricken upbringing had taken its toll, and he wondered if his Music Hall dream was nothing more than a wasted longing. His body ached at the joints, he was hungry and thirsty, and had been marching up and down Shaftsbury Avenue all morning and was now as parched as dry toast, and the July sun in the cloudless sky brought him nothing but discomfort and misery, as it did most of London's underprivileged. His current employers insisted he walked Shaftsbury Avenue most of the day, alternating the south side with the north side. The pay was poor, but at least it was a job, and he was paid at the end of each day when he returned to their premises by the Thames embankment near Charing Cross at six in the evening. But the demanding walk in the sweltering city exhausted him, and left him scant energy to pursue his ambition to be a Music Hall entertainer. Several evenings a week he sang in pubs, where he managed to earn a few coppers, sometimes as much as a shilling if the customers felt charitable. But mostly it was pennies, and it was only on rare occasions did the meagre coppers add up to a shilling. In order to survive, he tramped the strength-sapping streets, advertising a patented fabric cleaner on his front and back. But it wasn't just the need of money that kept him tramping the streets. He spent the time thinking, racking his brains for the right words. Words that might one day transport him from barroom to theatre. If only he could write that one memorable song that would be his entry to the Music Halls.

Suddenly, amid the cacophony of the busy street, a rasping voice startled him, close to his ear. 'Where d'you put the mustard, Bill?'

He turned round carefully, hampered as he was by his sandwich board and stared at the owner of the abrasive voice. He recognised him as a neighbour, one of the residents from Little Dublin in the St Giles area.

'Don' you remember me?' the man grinned through blackened teeth. 'Name's Tom. I sees you goin' out early this mornin' an' I says to myself, there goes a man looking' to fill a sandwich, an' I wonders where the mustard goes.'

Bill stared unblinkingly at the man and replied, 'If I 'ad a farthing for every one who throws that one my way... '

The man gave a throaty chuckle and finished the sentence for him. 'You'd be living in clover.'

Bill nodded mournfully and stared at the man's rodent-like face. He remembered seeing him once in Lumber Court, buying old clothes. Then, more recently, he thought he remembered seeing him at the Red Lion.

The man grinned knowingly. 'Saw you the other night at the Red Lion.'

Bill felt unnerved, thinking the man might be some sort of mind reader. One of those psychics who were all the rage.

'Wothca make after you pushed the hat round?'

'Eight pence and three farthings. Not much when you think I had to share it with the pianist.'

The man shook his head and made a whistling sound through the gaps in his teeth. 'Tell you what: you look in need of refreshment. What do you say I stand you a pint at this little alehouse I know just off Frith Street.'

Bill tried to look into the man's eyes without narrowing his own. He was suspicious. His first instinct was one of distrust. Even though the offer seemed genuine, the man's hearty manner seemed excessive. He behaved as if they were old friends, yet Bill had only ever seen him – well, perhaps on more than those two occasions. Hadn't he seen him ducking and diving in their insalubrious neighbourhood? But then most of the impecunious residents had reason to dodge creditors, especially landlords, as Bill himself had reason to on many occasions.

Noticing his hesitation, the man clicked his tongue and let his impatience grow. 'Well, what's it to be? I haven't got all day.'

'I didn't mean to be rude,' Bill explained. 'But my employers insist I walk up and down Shaftsbury Avenue the whole day. They may check up on me from time to time. And if I'm not here, and I happens to shirk my work in Soho, 'stead of—'

The man's attitude changed deftly into one of sympathy and concern. He placed a hand on Bill's shoulder and smiled. 'I understand, my old china. But surely they can't begrudge you a short break to quench your thirst on a hot day like today.'

Bill had to admit the offer was tempting. He had just enough in his pocket for a pint of ale and a pie for when he finished work, so the offer of a free glass of sustaining beer would keep him going for the next four hours.

'And I feel guilty,' the man added, waiting for Bill to ask what he meant.

Bill complied with a tilt of his head and another beard scratch. 'Guilty?'

‘When I saw you singing your heart out at the Red Lion, I never so much as dropped a farthing in the hat.’

‘Well,’ Bill began, ‘no one need feel obliged—’

‘No, but you was still working for pennies. That sort of entertainment should not be given on the house. I feel I owes you a drink for having shied away from the hat.

But I wus short of funds that night. So how about it?’

Bill glanced over his shoulder, although he didn’t expect to see anyone deliberately spying on him in the busy Avenue. ‘Very well. I will accompany you for a glass of ale but I had better not stay too long.’ Then, realising he had made it sound as if he was doing the man a favour rather than the other way round, added, ‘I am much obliged to you for a glass, welcome on such a day.’

The man gave him a wide grin, patted him on the shoulder, and guided him into Soho. They crossed Dean Street into Frith Street and found a small unsavoury-looking public house in one of Soho’s back streets. As soon as they stepped inside the pub, into the gloomy smoke-filled den where the sun never reached, the burly, stubble-chinned landlord scowled at Bill.

‘You ain’t bringing sandwich boards in here. No room. ‘Sides, I ain’t got the mustard to go wiv ‘em.’

Bill stopped in the open doorway. ‘What am I gonna do? I can’t leave it outside. Someone might—’

‘Half-inch sandwich boards?’ the landlord laughed. ‘No one ain’t got a hankerin’ for sandwich boards. Leave it outside the door, if you wanna drink.’

Bill hesitated, while his beer benefactor knocked the back of the board with his knuckles and said, ‘Come on, matey, you know he’s right. Ain’t no one got a need for sandwich boards. An’ who gives a tinker’s curses for patented fabric cleaner?’

Bill backed into the street and, helped by his new friend, raised the sandwich boards from his aching shoulders. He leant the placards against the wall, so that half of the boards could be seen through the open doorway from the inside of the pub.

But his friend moved them to one side so they were no longer visible from the bar.

‘Hey! What are you doing? I won’t be able to keep me eye on ‘em now.’

‘Can’t block the entrance, matey. Come on, let’s have that drink.’

He was ushered towards the bar, and while they waited for the landlord to pour two pints of ale, Bill glanced nervously over his shoulder towards the street.

A hand patted his shoulder.

‘Relax, matey. Enjoy the beer.’

They clinked glasses and drank. Bill had forgotten just how thirsty he was and tilted the glass, downing most of the pint in one open-throated swallow. But as he drank, he saw the crafty smirk on his companion’s face, who winked at the landlord as if they shared a secret joke. Noticing the suspicious expression on Bill’s face, his companion explained with a nod towards the landlord, ‘We ain’t seen such swallowing since Elephant Lil won the yard of ale competition. That’s what tickled us. Elephant Lil and the yard of ale. Cor, what a sight that was.’

Reassured by the reference to this renowned Soho event, and suddenly feeling light headed, Bill said, ‘I hadn’t noticed how thirsty I was.’ He giggled, and was about to swallow the last of his beer when his companion stopped him with a grubby hand on his.

‘Only a measure of three fingers left in the glass. Have another, matey.’

Bill looked nervously towards the door. ‘I really ought—’ he began.

‘Nonsense. Get it down you and ‘ave another. It’ll make the rest of the day go quicker. As quick as you can drink, if I’m not mistaken. Fill er’ up, landlord.’

Bill drank the rest of the beer and placed his glass on the bar. ‘I’m much obliged to you. But are you not joining me?’

The man laughed, giving Bill another glimpse of his rotten teeth. ‘I ain’t as fast imbibing as some people.’ He gave the landlord another conspiratorial wink. ‘But I’ll soon speed up, and a glorious guzzling I’ll have for the rest of the afternoon.’

Although Bill had been offered the second pint, the landlord ignored his empty glass and moved along the bar to serve another customer. Bill shifted uncomfortably from one foot to another. It had been a long day so far, and now the liquid weighed heavily on his bladder. 'I think I may need to relieve myself.' He threw an anxious look at the street, hoping his sandwich board was still safe.

His companion patted him on the shoulder. 'You're worried 'bout your boards, ain't yah? Tell you what: while you're making room for another beer, I'll pop out an' make sure all's well, then you can relax and 'ave the other beer wiv me.'

Bill smiled gratefully. 'I am so obliged. So much in your debt.'

The man placed a hand on his heart. 'On the contrary, it is I who am indebted to you, sir, for such great entertainment.'

Bill hurried off to the pub's lavatory to relieve himself, singing a comic song as he did so. He felt content, and told himself he had been foolish in not trusting a man willing to treat him to pints of beer because his singing was appreciated. Why distrust a man who wanted nothing more than companionship? As he returned to the bar, he felt a renewal of optimism and brotherly love. But as he walked through the adjoining door leading from the lavatory, he couldn't see his companion anywhere in the bar. A suspicious bolt shot through his body. He dashed towards the pub entrance and stepped out into the street. The wall where he had stood his placards was bare. The sandwich boards had gone.

Panicking, he went back into the pub and approached the landlord, who was talking to another customer.

'The man I was with. Where is he?'

The landlord pursed his lips, shrugged, ignored Bill and continued talking to the customer.

'What am I going to do? My sandwich board is gone!' Bill screamed. 'The bastard has taken it. He said he'd look after it and he's taken it.'

The landlord pointed a stubby finger at Bill. 'Hoy! You ain't having no barney in my pub. You can buy a drink or you can clear off.'

Despair swamped Bill's voice as he came close to tears. 'But where is he?' he croaked. 'Where did he go?'

'How should I know. He just stepped out the door.'

'You know him, don't you?'

'Never seen him before in my life.'

'Yes, you do. I could tell.'

'You calling me a liar?'

Bill's eyes blazed with sudden anger. 'Yes! You're lying. You're both in it together. You're a liar and a cheat.'

'What did you say?' The landlord picked up a cudgel from under the bar and moved towards the counter flap.

'All right! I'm going. I'm going.'

As Bill skedaddled across the bar and back into the street, he heard the landlord yelling after him, 'And don't come back!'

He moved a few yards away from the pub, then stopped, looking up and down the street in both directions. The cheating bastard would be long gone by now, and Soho was full of little alleys and courts down which a man could disappear if chased. How could he have been so stupid as to fall for that one? He'd been set up, that was for sure. The man had taken his sandwich board and would probably paint over the fabric advertisement and then sell it to another company for them to advertise their wares. For the cost of a few pennies outlay for the beer, the man might make a reasonable profit, selling the sandwich boards for as much as five or ten shillings. And, Bill suspected, the deal may have been agreed on in advance, with the thief offering his services to an unscrupulous buyer, saying he might be able to provide the goods for such and such a price. Find the buyer before obtaining the goods, which was what many thieves in the corrupt city did. Street sharp enough to know how this worked, Bill had still been the dupe of the deception, and cursed himself for his stupidity. He should have listened to his first instincts.

As he ambled slowly along the narrow street, he felt as if imaginary sandwich boards hung on his shoulders. The imaginary weight was his wishful thoughts, and his steps got shorter as he walked in a trance, wondering where to go or what to do next.

He could not now go to his employers and admit the sandwich boards had been stolen. They would want to know why. Perhaps he could explain that he had to take them off to relieve himself. But, they would argue, why had he not walked back down Haymarket and across Trafalgar Square to their premises – only a ten or fifteen minute walk – as they told him to do whenever that situation arose? After all, the message of his boards could still be seen by hundreds of prospective buyers whether he was in Trafalgar Square or Shaftsbury Avenue.

He reached the corner of Frith Street, halted at the edge of the kerb and came face to face with a horse. The bedraggled creature, harnessed into a cart delivering ice to a restaurant, stared at him with indifference; but so wound up was he from the recent encounter with the black toothed swindler, he interpreted the horse's impartial gaze as the baleful focus of an evil entity. He walked hurriedly along Frith Street, deciding he would spend his last remaining coins in the snug of the Dog and Duck, while contemplating his future.

He managed to find a corner seat, spent the last of his money on beer and a meat pie, and settled down to brood upon his circumstances. He had offered to sing that night at a pub in Islington, which would be a long walk but he wanted to meet with the pianist, someone who had offered to write the music for some of his songs, unfortunately he hadn't yet come up with the comic song that would be his entrée to the Halls. But his output was far from prolific, consisting of only three songs – one about a lady's little lapdog, one about a six-legged cat, and a sentimental ballad about a chimney sweep's boy. None of which had set the pubs ablaze with enthusiasm, so he mostly sang other well-known comic songs and ballads, even resorting to Robert Herrick's 'Cherry Ripe' on occasions.

After he had eaten his pie, he sipped his beer slowly to make it last, took out his notebook and pencil and stared at a blank sheet, willing himself to think of something he could show the pianist that evening. But his mind was as blank as the page. He blamed lack of inspiration on his recent misfortune. Of all the dastardly deeds, stealing a poor sandwich man's boards had to be the worst, the pettiest crime imaginable. And then, as he thought about the missing sandwich boards and mellowed slowly with each sip of ale, an idea formed in his brain, slight at first, then growing into a magnificent vision of a comic song. He scribbled a few words, and then a few more. A smile tugged at the corners of his mouth as he scribbled furiously, composing a song with the most memorable chorus he had ever known. Suddenly he felt nothing but gratitude towards the blackguard with the black teeth. Had the man not swindled him he might not now be inspired to sit in the Dog and Duck composing a song which might one day be sung in every parlour throughout the land and bring him fame and fortune. 'Thank you, you black hearted blackguard,' he spoke aloud. 'Thank you for giving me the inspiration I needed.'

That evening, feverish with excitement, he showed the pianist his new song, and they arranged to meet the next day. A day later, the song was tried out at one of the better pubs in the City Road, and for the first time one of Bill Flintlock's songs received thunderous applause and cries for more. The song was repeated and received another rapturous ovation. Before long, Bill was singing it in minor music-hall theatres in Soho, and by the end of the summer he was second on the bill at Wilton's Music Hall. He wrote many more songs, all of them reasonably good, and within two years the public's appetite grew on the songs he wrote. He toured the British Isles, happily travelling First Class by railway, glad he rarely had to look another horse in the eye. And from his growing Music Hall repertoire there was always one song the audience demanded, which became a firm favourite throughout the land. Full of subtle innuendo, metaphors and puns, the song was about a sandwich man and was called 'Where Do You Put Your Mustard, Bill?' It sold more sheet music than any other song during Queen Victoria's last reigning year.

Down And Out

We found Kevin Clacton sleeping rough in a Carnaby Street shop doorway talking to a dessert spoon which he held in his hand as if it was one of his old club microphones. Usually the down and outs, the druggies and the alcoholics, gravitate towards the mainline stations, Charing Cross being the nearest to Soho, where you'll always find some poor unfortunate sprawled out in a grubby sleeping bag near the Underground ticket office, a few begged-for coins in a hat or cardboard box. But we'd never seen Kevin at any of the railway stations before; he suddenly appeared at the Carnaby Street doorway, talking gibberish at his spoon, so we guessed he was a recent fall from a more illustrious life.

I'm a social worker, and we do our best to help the homeless – mostly men, though there are quite a few women on the streets. Most of the homeless, when they're tired and hungry, and they've run out of funds for alcohol or drugs, arrive at the Soho church hall where we distribute donated sandwiches, about to reach their sell-by date, and hot beverages. The Carnaby Street shop proprietor telephoned us and asked if we would remove Kevin from their doorway before they opened for business one morning. We brought him in to the church hall and could see by the still reasonable state of his clothes that he hadn't long been sleeping rough. Unlike many of our service users, he didn't reek of alcohol, and I thought he probably had mental problems brought about by some tragic event. It was difficult to guess his age; he could have been forty or sixty, it was impossible to tell, as it is with most vagrants sleeping rough.

As soon as he'd been given a breakfast, we had one of our group therapy sessions and Kevin immediately responded positively, although he became impatient having to sit and listen to others, but when it was his turn I could see it was going to be a long drawn out tale. Many of our service users are reluctant to speak about their problems, but not Kevin. I always sit everyone in a circle, but Kevin ignored this protocol and leapt up clutching his spoon like it was wired for sound, standing slightly outside the circle, hogging the limelight. He told us he was a stand-up comedian, and when he saw what he thought was a sneering expression of disbelief on the face of someone in the group, he became aggressively defensive. He had a strong memory of who he used to be, one minute he would lucidly reveal the story of his life, and the next minute he suddenly veered into a ranting caricature of his former self as he attempted to recall the taglines to his endless string of dirty jokes. I could see his desperation and madness as he stood up and began speaking, clutching his spoon like a comfort blanket.

'Testing, testing, testing. One, two three, four,' he said to the imaginary microphone. 'There was this nun feeding pigeons outside the convent.' Someone in the group whispered something and Kevin glared at them and shouted, 'So what's wrong if I start off with a few sure-fire gags? You got a problem with that?'

'Kevin!' I said 'Calm down. Just tell us about what happened to you before we found you in Carnaby Street.'

'Sorry, Doc,' he said sheepishly, bowing his head in an exaggerated parody of a penitent. I thought of telling him I wasn't a doctor, and giving him my name yet again, but didn't think it would do much good.

'OK, Kevin. Carry on.'

'We all know why we're here,' he said with a slight smile. 'I just thought it was time you heard it from someone who was unashamedly successful. Kevin Clacton's the name! And laughter's the game!' He delivered this line to old Margo the wino who stared at him open-mouthed. 'Sounds corny, you're thinking. So I wait for one of you to heckle.'

He paused, looking round the group as if he expected someone to oblige. There were ten of them in the group, all men apart from Margo, and they were confused. Apart from Sam, a young drug addict, who giggled as though only he had a secret grasp of

Kevin's act. Encouraged by Sam's response, Kevin continued his story.

'It don't matter a toss what you shout out, 'cos I always top it. I've got hundreds of heckler put-downs. None of 'em new, I'm the first to admit, but every one a winner. You've got to bear in mind, it's what made me a success. Yes! A success!' He glowered at the group as if someone had contradicted him, but no one had said a word. Young Sam nodded as if he understood, and this seemed to pacify Kevin. 'It was mostly stag nights and sweaty, smoky, dirty little clubs. And I know I've never been on the telly but listen to this.' Holding the spoon in his left hand, he counted off points with the fingers of his right. 'I had a six bedroom house near Westcliff-on-Sea; heated swimming pool in the garden, a beautiful blonde wife called Tina – an ex-Country and Western singer; a nine-year-old girl, Billie Jo, and a seven-year-old boy – Kevin Junior. We had three cars between us. A Merc, a Shogun and a little Renault run-around. So that's not bad is it, for someone what could walk down the road without being recognised? Everything I owned was pure gold. I couldn't stand nothing cheap and nasty. I've always said you get what you pay for in life. It was the same with Tina. Now there was a woman with looks *and* taste. And she could sing like Billie Jo Spears. I'll never forget our fifth anniversary. Know what she done?

She took me out on to the patio and played my favourite song on the stereo, 'Blanket On The Ground'. And when I looked out over the garden towards the pool, there in the shadows and dying embers of the barbecue, there *was* a blanket on the ground. Well, call me an old softie if you like, but I almost cried I was so moved.'

He stopped and his eyes became distant as he remembered, and then as if to erase the painful memories, he relapsed into his routine. 'There was this scoutmaster walking along the street, right. An' he sees this tart wiv enormous knockers.'

Sam laughed loudly and it was Kevin's turn to look confused.

'I ain't got to the tag yet, you moron.'

I raised my hand. 'Kevin, what do you say we take a little break here and continue this another time?'

He glared at me, and I saw how cornered and frightened he was. 'Sorry, Doc. Got carried away. You got to hear the rest of the story. The one about the comedian who couldn't get it up. Good joke that.'

I thought we were getting close to the truth now, and letting him tell his story might help him. So I nodded and he continued.

'There was this comedian and he knew enough dirty jokes to cover the karzy walls from 'ere to Land's End. And shall I let you into a secret? He never found them funny. And the less funny he found them, the more the punters laughed. And the more the punters laughed, the more he hated them. Life was just one big unfunny joke. But the worst joke of all was the one about the impotent comedian who came home to find his wife in bed wiv another bloke. Her hairdresser! I thought all them ladies' hairdressers batted for the other side. Not this one though. Right little Warren Beatty. Know what I mean? Like that film *Shampoo.* To look at this geezer you'd have sworn he was bent. There was something a bit feminine about him. The way he moved. I'd seen him once, when Billie Jo, Kevin Junior, Tina and me was out walking our pooch. He comes up and greets Tina gaily – if you know what I mean – like women do when they meet each other. But I reckon it was all part of his act, making out he was... when all the time he was... '

Kevin paused as if he'd lost his train of thought, or maybe it was a reluctance to face the rest of his wretched history. And whenever he got close to the painful truth, I noticed, he spoke in the third person, like some comedic alter ego was telling the story. Suddenly, he realised he might have paused for too long and he felt the group becoming restless.

'Sorry, Doc,' he said. 'The story gets better now. What you've all been waiting for. The bedroom scene. The comedian has a gig cancelled and comes home early. They might have heard his car pull up if it hadn't been for one of the neighbours mowing the lawn. Normally, whenever he got home, the comedian would call out to say he was back. But for some reason he didn't that day. He goes into the lounge to get himself a vodka and tonic. Opening the cocktail cabinet might have spooked them out upstairs. A bespoke cabinet. Plays a medley of the country greats. But he didn't open it that day. I've no idea why. Oh yes, I do. Maybe he decided to go into the kitchen to get some ice. So he just stopped

– stood there listening. And that was when he heard this sound from upstairs, like someone was in pain. He knew exactly what that was about and his blood ran cold.'

'Just a minute! Just a minute!' Sam interrupted the narrative. 'You said you had children – Billie Jean and... '

'Jo!' Kevin snapped.

I could see him becoming flustered.

'Yeah, whatever,' Sam said. 'So where was your kiddies when this was going on?'

'I can't fucking remember.' Kevin studied his distorted reflection on the back of the spoon as he thought about this. 'Yes, I can. It was a Friday afternoon. I think. My gig was up north, and I wasn't many miles away from home when I got a call on my mobile to tell me it was off. The kids I remembered were at a birthday party.'

'So you went upstairs and caught them at it,' Sam said with undisguised glee.

'Who's telling this?'

'You are, Kevin,' I said. 'Go on with your story. Get it off your chest.'

Kevin paused briefly as he tried to recall that fateful day. 'Anyway, I takes the stairs three at a time. Quietly, so I could surprise them. They thought I was two hundred miles away so they'd left the bedroom door open. So I walks in, bracing myself for the worst. And, sure enough, what I saw was the hairy arse of the hairdresser pounding away on top of my missus, well into the final furlong, and all that disgusting moaning and groaning as they reach the short strokes.'

I could see Kevin becoming agitated, the way he perspired with veins standing out on the side of his head. It was then I guessed that telling his story in the third person may have been a safety valve. Now it was in the first person he was forced to face his demons and I wondered how he would cope. Certainly the rest of the service users were all attentive, enjoying the narrative like a television programme.

Kevin wiped the flat of his hand over his face before continuing. 'At first they didn't see me in the doorway, so I coughs. Should have seen them jump. Broke apart like two startled dogs. So what did I do? I kept my cool. Walked over to the dressing table, picked up a pair of scissors, grabbed my wife by the hair and started snipping away. "What are you doing?" she screams. "Well," I says, "your boyfriend's performing my function, so I thought I'd perform his." I waited for the laugh, but it never came. Instead, my missus screams, "Get him off me, Jason." And when the bastard tries to pull me off, I let him have it in the guts with the scissors. "Does it hurt?" I asked, while the hairdresser sinks to the floor, blood flowing like claret. "You're supposed to say *only when I laugh!*" But he didn't appreciate the joke. He weren't injured that bad. Not as much as I was, cos Tina ends up marrying him. And I end up in the funny farm.'

The end of his sad tale was followed by a smattering of applause, started by Sam. My assistant Jan, sitting next to him, stopped him with a hand on his, and the applause trickled out. But Kevin appeared not to notice as he addressed me, his face tense and tormented..

'You know, they say guns or knives don't kill people. It's husbands who come home early who kill people. And looking back on it, that's what I should've done. I should've topped the bastard. Just for my own piece of mind. But I get confused, and the only way I can stop myself feeling anything is to numb the pain with jokes I never found funny. So what's it all about, Doc, eh? Just one great big bowl of cherries or shit? Take your pick. You're lookin' at a man who likes to make 'em laugh. But sometimes my head's so crowded it hurts. Crammed full of jokes it is. And there's no room for anything else. All my life I've told jokes on stage, in pubs and clubs and bars, for money and for free. People laugh, but all my life I've never found them funny. But I need to tell 'em, cos without them I'm nothing. I don't exist.'

'Thank you, Kevin,' I began. 'That was a very brave... ' I stopped as he suddenly moved towards me. At first I thought he was going to flip and I braced myself, preparing for a violent outburst, but he stopped in the centre of the circle and looked me in the eye.

'Sorry, doctor, but you might have to chalk this up as one of your failures.' He spun round and addressed the group in general. 'If you enjoyed my little spot, please tell your friends. If you haven't, keep your mouths shut!' He turned back to me. 'And now I'll let you introduce the next failure. See you around.'

Still clutching his spoon, he marched quickly towards the exit. I nodded to Jan, getting her to take over the group, while I chased after Kevin, worried about his mental state.

'Kevin! Hang on, mate!' I called, but he was already out the door. I followed and I saw him crossing the green and heading towards Wardour Street. After his cogent description of his failed marriage, I could see he had reverted to the shield of his madness as he stepped into the street, speaking loudly to his imaginary microphone.

'Testing, testing, testing. One, two, three, four.'

I saw people staring at him and moving hastily out of his way. I tried to catch up with him but he had already disappeared into an alley. And then I lost him, so I returned to the church hall.

Most of our service users we see from time to time. We know most of them by name. They are our regulars. Occasionally some of them are found dead unable to survive a harsh winter, while others disappear temporarily then resurface after having moved to another district in a haze. But not Kevin the stand-up comedian. We never saw him again, and I often wondered what became of him. To vanish so completely is unusual. But it's not unknown. We often get sent circulars asking if we have seen such and such a missing person, with a name and photograph. But never anything about Kevin, as if he had never existed.

I like to think he saw the funny side of his own history, took it to the Edinburgh Festival, and found a new lease of life as an alternative comedian. But I realise that's just a fantasy of mine.

Home To Roost

I

Mavis froze when she saw the arrival of the latest resident. She thought she recognized him, but it was nearly forty years ago and she could have been mistaken.

If it was him, he had put on an excessive amount of weight, and it took three of them – Mavis, the matron and another carer – to shift him from the van into one of the home's wheelchairs. The matron asked her what was wrong and she made a feeble excuse – said she was tired and feeling the strain.

As they manoeuvred him into the wheelchair, Mavis stared intently into his face to see if there was a trace of recognition. But there was nothing, and she wondered if she might be imagining it, haunted as she was by her past. Whenever she confronted her reflection in the mirror she often wondered what had become of the beauty of those early years, and she was aware that four decades can not only change a person physically but sometimes beyond recognition. So there was no telling if it was him or not. Yet there was something about the man, something she couldn't quite put her finger on. Just a feeling she had. He looked nothing like him, but she fancied she saw arrogance in his eyes, undimmed by the years and unchanged by senility.

As they wheeled him into the care home, she knew she would soon find out if her first instinct had been right, because after wheeling him into reception, matron would take him to her office to make the registration, and that's when she would find out his name. But what if the name he'd used all those years ago was an alias? She had no way of knowing. After all, he'd been the one to insist on her working under another name. Mavis was unglamorous, he said, so he renamed her and she became Jade. He told her it sounded more exotic. Not that she minded changing her name, it made what she did feel less real, as if it was something that happened to another person.

They left him parked in the wheelchair outside the office, and Mavis held the door open for the matron to deal with the registration, while the other carer dashed off to deal with a problem in the lounge where one of the many residents was showing signs of distress. Mavis looked down at the pathetic elderly sufferer in the wheelchair while she waited at the open door, examining every detail of his puffed, wrinkled and bloated face. Surely this couldn't be the same man, could it? Jake Jackman had been dark-haired and slim, with neat sideburns like Elvis, whereas this overweight lump of flesh was bald, with just a few wisps of grey hair clinging to the sides of his head like curling strands of cotton. She'd been told he was the victim of a massive stroke and stared into his eyes to see if there was a flicker of recognition. He made a loud spluttering noise and she jumped. She couldn't recognise it as speech, it was like the noise deaf people sometimes make, incoherent and loud. But the fact he had attempted some sort of communication meant there was something going on inside his head. She wondered if he had recognised her. If he had, what was it he was trying to say? Remorse for what he had done to her? She doubted that very much. Jake's only consideration had been for Jake and Jake alone.

The matron put away her notes in a desk drawer and said it was all done. She came and stood at the door and gave the man in the wheelchair the sort of smile reserved for children and pets. Mavis held her breath, waiting for the matron to speak to him, and reveal his name.

'We'll take you to your own room now, Graham,' Matron said. 'And after that we'll get you some nice tea.'

Graham! Perhaps it wasn't him. Perhaps she'd been mistaken. The anti-climax was overwhelming. For years she'd thought about revenge, wondering what she would do if she ever met him again. And it was a fantasy up until this moment. An occasional indulgence. Back then she was a vulnerable eighteen-year-old and he was in his late thirties. She was now in her late-fifties, and much healthier than she'd ever been. Hard work kept her occupied and in good shape. So that would make him seventy-something. Almost eighty. So she knew that if ever their paths crossed again she had nothing to fear. The man in the wheelchair certainly looked the right age. But his name was Graham. Not that it meant anything. After all, Mavis became Jade in an instant. So why couldn't Graham become Jake? But was this man in a near vegetative state him? Perhaps she had jumped to a faulty conclusion. Yet her first instinct had warned her that here was the cause of her misery. There was only one way she could find out for sure.

As they neared Room 16, where Mrs Omar had passed away ten weeks ago, which was to be the new resident's room, Mavis, lowered her voice as she spoke to the matron, making it sound like a half-interested enquiry, as if she was getting a more rounded identity of the man.

'Does Graham have a surname?' she whispered, aware the man in the wheelchair could probably hear every word.

'Yes, of course he does,' the matron replied, opening the door for Mavis to push in the wheelchair. Once they were inside the small neat room, the matron addressed the man jovially, though it was said for Mavis's benefit, in reply to her enquiry. 'Here we are, Mr Jackman. This is your own little room.'

Mavis imagined she could hear the screech of tyres, a car skidding to a halt. Time was suspended for an instant. Her breathing became shallow and she felt herself overheating. She clutched the back of the wheelchair for support and thought for a moment she might faint..

'You all right, Mavis?' said the matron. 'You look as if you've seen a ghost.'

Mavis's voice was hoarse when she replied. 'It's the heat. Makes me feel a bit woozy.'

'It's always the same temperature, Mavis. You know that.'

'I'll be fine. Just a sudden nauseous feeling, that's all. It'll pass.'

And it *had* passed. It was the initial shock. It was definitely him, she was sure of it now. Jackman. Her first reaction coupled with the surname was too much of a coincidence. It had to be him. It just had to be. And she couldn't imagine that swaggering Soho pimp using a suburban name like Graham. He had probably adopted a name with a tougher image. So if it was him – and she was sure it was – he was now the vulnerable one. After all these years, she had him right where she wanted him.

One of the porters arrived, coughing to announce his entrance, and bringing Jackman's belongings from the van. It was lunchtime and matron suggested that Mavis take Graham to the dining area just off the lounge and feed him, while she prepared his room and unpacked his clothes.

Mavis nodded dutifully. 'I look forward to that very much,' she said ominously, staring into Jackman's face, searching for any sign of an understanding. She wheeled him to the dining area and parked his wheelchair at an angle in front of one of the dining tables. One of the kitchen staff, an Asian woman, her head covered in a purple scarf, brought a plate of mashed potatoes, fish in white sauce and peas and placed it on the table. Mavis mashed up a small mound of the food with the back of a fork, scooped a little mound of it on to a spoon, and moved it slowly towards Jackman's mouth. He opened his mouth to accept the offering, his lips moving up and down eagerly like a fledgling bird. Mavis stopped, holding the spoon inches from his mouth. She saw panic in his eyes, and smiled heartlessly, enjoying the feeling of power she held over this useless lump of flesh. *You know who I am don't you, you bastard?* She put the spoon back on the plate and leant forward to talk to him quietly, their heads close like two conspirators.

'Remember me, Jake?' She saw the comprehension in his eyes, a flicker of alarm. 'Oh, yes, you bastard, you know fuckin' well, don't you? I've got you just where I want you. You are not getting away from me. You are going to suffer for what you done to me.'

II

Jackman's cramped Soho flat was on the top floor of a ramshackle building in a narrow passageway which ran between Wardour Street and Dean Street, with a red telephone box which stood sentinel at one end of the alley. Inside the box, the space above the telephone was plastered with postcards offering the delights of Trudi, Amber, Candy and countless other call girls; one only had to pick up the phone and dial to experience the guilty pleasures of what has moved the world since time began. At the centre of the alley was a shop window, lit up with a neon sign and the simple message 'sex'. Displayed under the sign on boxes covered with fading magenta crepe paper was a display of luridly-titled videos and magazines, and a mannequin dressed in bondage leather stood in a corner of the window, peering through a mask with lifeless eyes, whip in hand. On the opposite side of the entrance to the sex shop was a permanently open door, and a notice on the frame scrawled with felt-tip pen in red offered the delights of a euphemistically named 'model' on the first floor, instructing the customer to ring the bell before ascending. The staircase was narrow, uncarpeted and each stair creaked loudly like the sound effect from a horror film. On the second floor lived the landlord who sublet the first floor flat on a pro rata basis to whichever pimp or call girl needed a working premise for a few hours or days, depending on whether or not trade was busy. Above his flat on the top floor was Jackman's two- room flat, and he had often toyed with the idea of using it for the same purposes as his landlord, but it was clearly out of the question, since his landlord wouldn't entertain any competition in the same building. So the flat was just somewhere for Jackman to sleep, although he often woke late, then spent what was left of the morning studying the form for the day's racing, before going out and spending the rest of the day at the bookmaker's and pubs. He occasionally made forays by train to race meetings, but more often than not he stuck to Soho like a ship's barnacle. He was an inveterate gambler, although he tried to confine himself to horses, kidding himself there was a science in studying the form, the weights, the handicaps. He bet heavily, and would sometimes win enormous amounts of money, but often he would crash and burn, and end up having to borrow hugely, paying back money borrowed at extortionate rates of interest. During the down times he thought about how advantageous it would be to find an accommodating young girl willing to be exploited. If only he could find this buffer from his losses, a guaranteed income. Unfortunately, he knew only too well that if he was lucky enough to find a willing meal ticket, there were other men in Soho – men with connections – he didn't dare challenge. These were influential hoodlums and it was dangerous to muscle in on their territory and rackets. So he abandoned any hope of living off a girl's immoral earnings – certainly as far as Soho was concerned.

But whenever he was flushed from winnings, and feeling horny, he liked to visit more exclusive call girls in Mayfair's Shepherd Market. These were the high class prostitutes whose clientele were streets away from the shabby losers who climbed the stairs to the first floor of his Soho building. And once, on one of his many visits to Shepherd Market, he thought he recognised a member of parliament leaving his favourite call girl's flat. It was after these Mayfair visits that he dreamt his dream. He became ambitious. Not for him a seedy little Soho room with a naked red light bulb. One day, he promised himself, when he was on a roll, he would find the perfect floozy and set her up in Mayfair. But he needed a bird with film star looks. A stunner A Diana Dors look-alike, maybe. But, as the days turned into weeks, and the weeks into months, his avaricious and licentious dreams became as threadbare as the carpet in his flat. Until one day, when his dreams had all but popped like a soap bubble, he bumped into Mavis. .

After a traumatic childhood in Ipswich, growing up in a strict Catholic orphanage, Mavis escaped to London on her eighteenth birthday, and swore she would never look back, never go to church and never have children of her own. In spite of her scarred upbringing, Mavis was stunningly good looking, and because she had never been indulged like loved and spoilt children, her figure was perfectly proportioned and temptingly sensual. She was a natural blonde with high cheekbones, sparkling blue eyes, and turned men's heads wherever she walked. When Jackman spotted her wandering aimlessly around Piccadilly Circus one evening, staring wistfully at the flashing neon lights, he knew he'd found his gravy train. But he was smart enough to realise he couldn't leap in with his Mayfair proposition and needed to bide his time. Discovering she had only six pounds between solvency and destitution, and flushed from a good day at the bookies, he treated her to a slap-up meal at an Italian restaurant in Greek Street. During the meal he discovered she had nowhere to stay, having arrived at Liverpool Street station that very day carrying a heavy suitcase, which she had booked in at a left luggage bureau before taking the tube train to Piccadilly. He offered her a room for the night, then accompanied her to pick up her suitcase, and hired a taxi to bring her back to his Soho flat. He expected her to make some sort of objection to the location of the flat, seeing as it was above a sex shop and a flat of prostitution, but although she ascended the stairs with fear and apprehension, his generosity and understanding dispelled her dismay once she was settled in his flat.

That first night he was cunning enough to play the considerate charmer, and they drank gins and tonics way into the night. She told him about her life at the orphanage, and he detected the bitterness and her inclination to escape her past, and knew he could play on her desire to lead a more exciting life. As the alcohol freed her inhibitions, she admitted she wasn't a virgin, having been sexually abused by a male member of staff at the orphanage ever since she was fourteen-years-old. Now Jake, as he called himself, subtly suggested they made a move into the bedroom, and told her he would respect her and understand if she didn't want to have sex with him. It worked. He knew she felt she was in his debt, and had only one thing to offer, to pay him back for his generosity.

The very next day he asked her if she would start taking the birth pill, and because she didn't want to give birth to an unwanted child, she readily agreed. For weeks she was happy. And so was he, thinking that he might have fallen for her. But the biggest part of him was absorbed by his own needs and desires which came before anything else, and he spent most of his days gambling, leaving her alone in the flat, returning late in the evening to satisfy his own cravings. Mavis spent so long on her own in the small flat, she became bored and restless. She felt as trapped as she had in the holy sisters' orphanage and wanted to escape. Twice in their first month together he took her with him to the races, once to Folkestone and then to Kempton Park, but these two outings only swelled her discontent, giving her a teasing taste of freedom, freedom from the claustrophobic atmosphere of the shabby Soho flat. Occasionally, after a day gambling in Soho bookies, he returned in the evening and took her on pub crawls, where she developed a craving for gin. But mostly these outings were infrequent, and she became frustrated and resentful, although she tried to curb her feelings, knowing she was being supported by him, and the only thing she had to offer in return was the sex he demanded when he returned from the betting shops and pubs at night. So, although she became dependent on him, she determined that one day soon she would rouse herself and perhaps get a job, although she had no qualifications or work experience. And, as the days slipped by, nothing changed. She was torn between wanting something better and the debt she owed her saviour.

Jake, on the other hand, was content with things as they were. After all, she seemed to bring him luck. Most of the horses he chose romped first past the post, and by the end of their first month together he was richer by five-hundred pounds, a substantial sum in the mid-Seventies.

And then the honeymoon period came to an abrupt end.

As soon as she heard his feet tramping up the narrow stairs one evening, she could tell by the defeated tread and scrape of his soles on the curling linoleum outside the door that a great change had come about and things might never be the same again. As he entered the small living room, with its shabby alcove kitchen, she could tell he'd lost everything. She could tell by the slump of his shoulders, and the way his eyes darted guiltily away from her probing stare.

'How much have you last, Jake?' she demanded.

Exhausted by the trauma of wiping out five hundred pounds in less than two hours, he collapsed into a mangy armchair. He let his head tilt back and stared at the ceiling, his eyes vacant but his mind replaying the recent events of a gambler's what might have been if only he'd bet on his first choice.

'You had as much as five hundred quid, Jake. Don't tell me you lost it all.'

He sat up suddenly, leaned forward and glared at her. 'I need a drink.' He stared pointedly at the empty gin bottle. 'You've fucking drunk it all.'

'I was depressed. Knowing you'd blow everything.'

'Don't use my bad luck as an excuse. You're becoming a fucking lush, sweetheart. There was half a bottle left in that. You've done half a bottle in less than two hours.'

He stood up, eyes puffed with anger, and she thought for a minute he was going to hit her. But he restrained himself and sat at the table opposite her, on the chair with the wonky leg. He dropped his head into his hands and sighed.

'Christ! I'm sorry, sweetheart. I was on a roll. I could've cleaned up. It was the last race I bet on... the fucking favourite in a three horse race... lost by half a length. Half a fucking length! No one could have seen that one coming. I was up nearly two grand, and I could have come away with three.'

Her mouth fell open and her eyes widened. It was incredible. How could he be so stupid? Up by as much as two thousand pounds and he goes and throws it back at the bookies. 'I can't believe how stupid you are,' she snapped. 'The only winners are the bookies.'

He glared at her, hating her and her truth. 'Tell me something I don't know. And whose fucking money was it anyhow? It's not as if it was yours. Who bought that gin you drunk?' He jabbed an angry thumb at his breastbone. 'I did. That's who. I pay the rent for this gaff, and I've been providing you with food and drink. I've even give you money to buy clothes.'

'I'll pay you back, Jake. Soon as I get a job.'

He laughed harshly. 'Oh yeah? What you gonna work as? Barmaid? How much d'you think you'll earn as a barmaid or a waitress?' Suddenly, he stared at her with a glint in his eyes and his mouth widened into a broad grin. 'I've got a better idea. A much better idea of how you can earn good money.'

She knew exactly what he was driving at and thought about the women who plied their trade on the first floor of the building. Shaking her head rapidly, she said, 'If you think you can put me downstairs with those filthy... '

He didn't let her finish. His grin broadened as he placed a hand over hers and squeezed. 'Relax, sweetheart. I wouldn't wish that on my worst enemy. No, I've got other plans for you and me, baby.'

Over the next few weeks he borrowed enough money from a loan shark to put down a deposit for a small Mayfair flat, and then he coaxed her, begged her, and threatened her. Eventually, she reluctantly agreed, and she was put to work with him as her pimp and protector. At first, he promised she would do no more than two tricks a day for well-heeled clients, but his gambling habit needed supporting, so she had to resort to five men a day. She was now swept into his circle of increasing debt. Then, one day, her nightmares began.

Usually, Jake arranged the client visits, and made certain he was nearby in case she needed help. Most of her clients were either married, and even if they weren't they were the sort of men who demanded total discretion, and most of them probably had family commitments at weekends. Therefore, as in the title of the Greek film, Mavis -

or Jade as she was now known as – never worked on a Sunday, and Jake usually took her out for lunch, or she would go shopping in Oxford Street. But this one particular Sunday, when she awoke, Jake was gone. At first, she thought he had gone out to buy milk or the *News of the World,* as he occasionally did on a Sunday morning; but by late afternoon there was still no sign of him. And then the doorbell rang. Usually, clients announced themselves, saying they had an appointment at a certain time, and she would remotely unlatch the street door for them. But this was a Sunday and she wasn't expecting any clients. Unless Jake had gone out, got pissed and lost his key.

She clicked the speaker entry and asked who it was.

‘ Jade, I’m a friend of Jake’s. He asked me to call round to collect you. And bring you for surprise birthday party.’

She had no idea when it was Jake’s birthday, and had no reason to doubt the man, so she pressed the button to open the door to the building, and waited near the flat door for the man to climb the four flights to the second floor. She heard several footsteps, wondering why there was more than one person, and she was suddenly afraid. Something was not quite right. She began to open the door slowly and peered cautiously through the gap. That was when the door flew open, hitting her in the shoulder. There were two of them, and they shoved her backwards, entered the flat and slammed the door behind them.

Her life ended at the moment. She was slapped, cried out and was told it would be worse if she didn’t shut up. She cried silently, tears streaming down her cheeks like rainwater. They were large men, overweight but strong, with cruel faces and foreign accents. Through her heaving sobs she asked for Jake, but the men just laughed, telling her he owed them money. She now belonged to them. Jake had sold her to them to clear his debt.

That was when one of them held her down while the other took out a syringe and injected a vein in her arm. She thought it might be something to put her to sleep, and she begged them to stop. But instead of passing out, she experienced a strange feeling of elation, an unreality wiping out her fears. But when they began to undress her roughly, she struggled and cried out. She was slapped again, and then both men raped her. She lost any sense of time, her life playing at a slower speed. She gave up struggling, and didn’t know whether the experience was a swirling dream or a nightmare. Horrific and illusory images propelled her towards loathing and self-hatred, and she wished herself dead. Everything became a blur as she felt herself becoming a discarded and useless heap of nothing. She couldn’t remember much of what happened later. She vaguely remembered staggering, being half-carried down the stairs. A hand gripping her tightly by the throat. A car journey. For how long she had no idea. Then stumbling down stone steps into a dank basement.

Ten years later she was still there, a slave to heroin and sex. She discovered the men who had brought her there were Maltese.

She knew Malta was an island but she had no idea where it was. It could have been in the South Pacific as far as she was concerned. There was another girl who was kept in another room in the damp sex-smelling basement, run by an older woman, who resembled one of the men who had brought her there. She guessed she might have been either the man's mother or an older sister.

She was forced to have sex with at least ten clients a day, minimum. She was given a small amount of money and allowed out to visit a pub or to shop for clothes now and again. Of course, she could have escaped, just walked away, got on a train and travelled to anywhere she chose within reasonable distance to London. But she was well and truly hooked on heroin. Besides, she didn't have a single person whom she could approach for help, not a single friend in the world.

Then, in the mid-eighties, the Soho basement where she was kept was raided, the Maltese gangsters were arrested and the brothel was shut down. Then began her long struggle in and out of rehab, visits to psychiatrists and social services, which wiped out almost another decade. Eventually, because of her hatred of Jake, the man she rightly blamed as the cause of her tragic existence for the last twenty years, she switched from self-loathing, and her anger was projected at the evil monster who sold her to pay his gambling debts. The anger gave her the strength to turn herself round, and she successfully kicked the heroin habit and became one of the more devoted employees at the care home.

But, on her day's off, she often thought about Jake, wondering what became of him. She also wondered what she would do to him should there paths ever cross again, and she sometimes fantasised about taking her revenge in the most brutal way.

III

Whenever Mavis approached Jake in the residents' lounge, he moaned incoherently and she wondered if this was from fear or guilt, because she was now convinced he remembered her. There was a certain depth of understanding in his eyes, even though he found it difficult to communicate.

She spent more time with him than with any of the other residents, and the matron thought it was because he was the most needy, and Mavis was merely trying to help him to adjust to the home and his condition.

After her first talk to him, while she fed him his lunch, she made it clear he would suffer for what he had done to her. But she had no idea of how she could make this man suffer any more than he did already. What could she do to him? Spit in his food before feeding him? Squeeze his balls hard when no one was watching. After all, if he cried out no one would know what he was trying to say. They would just think he was upset about his condition and his inability to communicate. Or when she did her night shift, perhaps she could enter Room 16 and keep him from sleeping. She had seen a television documentary where they showed sleep deprivation as one of the worst forms of torture.

. But, because of all the revenge fantasies in the past, seeking satisfaction at his expense seemed to have dissipated. She questioned how anyone could take revenge on this pathetic lump of flesh. Wasn't he suffering enough now, locked as he was inside his body, unable to fend for himself? Totally reliant on carers like her for everything. And yet... she still craved some sort of satisfaction. Then an idea came to her, something which seemed only right and proper. She sat herself close to him one quiet afternoon after many of the other residents were dozing or watching television and cleared her throat softly prior to speaking. She saw the wary look in his eyes and knew he could comprehend what was going on. So she began by speaking softly, telling him about her life outside the home.

'You know, Jake,' she said in a voice full of soft sympathy, 'I feel sorry for the way you're locked inside your head. I think it must be as bad as a jail sentence. If not worse. Yes, definitely worse. Even when someone is locked in a cell they can decide whether or not to get up and read a book or watch TV. Whereas you... you're stuck there in your head but unable to make any decisions yourself. None at all.'

She grinned to let him know she would enjoy tormenting him. He let out a loud whale cry and she saw the flicker of terror in his eyes. She patted his hand gently.

'It's all right, sweetheart, I'm not going to hurt you. Just talk to you, and tell you about my days.' Her voice soothing, she began to enjoy herself. This was her therapy now.

'Know what I done on my day off last week, Jake? Did a bit of window shopping, then I went into Starbucks and had a hot chocolate and cake. Sat there for as long as I pleased and read a book. That's what freedom's all about, ain't it? Being free to do what you want, when you want. It was such a lovely day. After that I went an walked in the park – watched the children playing, some kids feeding ducks at the lake – and although nothing much was happening, it was such a warm day, and I could appreciate just being alive and being able to walk around and please myself. An' you know what I done in the afternoon? Went to this friendly little boozer I know – nice little local it is – and I had a couple of glasses of white wine. I can do that now, see. I can enjoy a drink without feeling I need to go on the hard stuff. I drink moderately, sometimes go days without a drink – especially when I'm working. But that's the great thing about freedom, ain't it? You can please yourself and not have to rely on anyone. It must be terrible for you, Jake. Stuck in that chair all day, relying on others to feed you. And still knowing what's going on. Because you do know, don't you sweetheart? Only too well.'

She stared into his eyes and smiled. It was then that he let out an enormous, attention-seeking guttural cry, and for a moment she thought one of the other carers would come running over to see what was wrong. But the smiling, caring way Mavis rubbed Jake's cheeks tenderly and soothed him, dispelled any worries someone might have and let her get on with attending to her patient – the patient she appeared to care for more than any of the other residents..

'Yes, I know this upsets you, Jake, so I'm going to leave you now. And from tomorrow I won't be here for a week. I'm off on holiday. A glorious seaside break for a week. I can't wait to tell you all about it when I get back. You'll like that, won't you?'

But Mavis lied about the holiday. She would go no further from her Canning Town council flat than the local library, shops and pub. But she wasn't going to tell Jake that. She planned to torment him by using her imagination.

When she returned a week later, and saw him staring into space in the residents' lounge, a bull-bellow came from deep inside him as he spotted her walking towards him. She gave him a triumphant smile as she got closer, registering the alarm in his eyes. She pulled up a chair, sat close to him and patted his knee.

'There, there, Jake!' she giggled, enjoying the effective therapy of using her ingenuity to make his purgatory worse. 'I'm here now to tell you all about my holiday. I know you want to hear all about it. It was wonderful just walking along the beach, looking in rock pools. Watching kids flying kites, and the air was so clear and the sky so blue, with seagulls darting and swooping. And then, at the end of such free days, sitting outside a pub in the evening, sipping wine and having a meal. It's so wonderful to be free and able to please yourself, and not having to rely on others. It must be terrible to be in your condition. You know, while I was away, I thought of sending you a postcard, saying "wish you were here", but that would have been a lie. So I thought I'd save up all my news to share with you. I expect you enjoy hearing about how I love the freedom of my life now. As soon as I walk away from the care home, I can please myself what I do, because I'm independent, you see. Which is more than can be said for someone not a million miles from here. Oh, yes, there's something to be said for having the liberty to please yourself. Now, d'you want to hear about one of my little excursions. About a little boat trip I took?'

She paused, and watched the way he seemed to shrink into the fabric of his chair. She waited for the cry of pain, and sure enough his unintelligible trumpeting blasted out over the residents' lounge, alerting some of the other staff that perhaps something was wrong. But when the matron saw the way Mavis handled him, unruffled and sympathetic, she shook her head and smiled, knowing she could leave it in Mavis's capable hands.

As for Mavis, she was never sure if Jake's distress came from remorse, from his hostility towards her, or from the way she provoked and taunted him. But as far as anyone in the care home was concerned, the matron and most of the other staff all acknowledged that Mavis seemed to make a positive contribution to Mr Jackman's well being.

And no one knew any different.

Tricky Dickey

Sally Atkinson was overworked but felt it was bad luck to complain. She had started her own business at the beginning of the new millennium, and her reputation grew daily as the celebrity culture snowballed. She smiled at her assistant, as a cup of freshly brewed black coffee was placed on her desk, positioned carefully on a her favourite coaster, a facsimile of a 45 rpm Parlophone record of 'Love Me Do' by the Beatles.

'Thank you, Lucy. What time is this chap coming to see us?'

'His appointment's for eleven.'

'And his celebrity is... ?' Sally raised enquiring eyebrows at her assistant who shook her head.

'I thought you knew.'

Sally shrugged it off. 'We'll soon find out. It's quiet this morning for a change.'

As soon as she finished her sentence the telephone rang. 'I spoke too soon.'

Lucy walked across the large office to her own desk and picked up the extension. 'Star Repro,' she announced on a rising inflexion with a smile, which Sally had taught her to use, telling her a listener can feel you smiling. Then Sally watched as her assistant's demeanour changed, a performance of repentance for the benefit of her listener. 'Oh, dear! That is bad news. It's never happened before. We've always had excellent feedback about this particular Madonna. Excellent. I'm so sorry. If there's anything we can do... no, no, of course, I quite understand, and I'll speak to Sally about it... she's in a meeting at the moment.' Lucy threw her employer a helpless look of panic as she ate humble pie and cringed into the phone.

But Sally's expression was bland. She didn't like her reputation to be dented in any way, and she couldn't imagine what the problem was. She was in her mid-thirties, and had worked hard throughout the nineties as an assistant to a well-known casting director, which gave her the experience she craved. She knew she couldn't compete with the major casting directors if she set up her own casting agency, so she used her experience to found Star Repro, a lookalike agency, and rented premises in Wardour Street, not far from Pizza Express, so that potential clients would be impressed by Star Repro's address, bang in the heart of the film industry.

She listened intently as Lucy wound up the call with another so sorry apology, and unthinkingly gulped her coffee which was scalding hot. The sudden swelling blister on the roof of her mouth didn't help her sinking mood.

'Well?' she demanded from her assistant. 'What was that all about?'

'That function in the City.'

'The major bank?'

'That's the one. Madonna got hammered and disgraced herself.'

'Huh!' Sally pouted. 'I can't believe those city slickers – not known for their sobriety – would be upset by our lookalike getting plastered.'

'It was when they commented on her singing badly at the karaoke... '

With a wave of the hand, Sally interrupted impatiently. 'She's a lookalike for Christ sakes. She *mimes* to Madonna records. She can't sing. I thought I made that clear to them. If they wanted a singing Madonna they should have booked the real one. Let's face it, just ten per cent of bank staff bonuses of ten per cent of the staff would have paid for Madonna herself to do a gig there.'

Lucy giggled nervously. 'Ah! That was the problem apparently. Our own sweet Madonna freaked out when they booed her singing, and when the song ended she accused them of fraudulent behaviour and went on about their bonuses with a stream of bad language.'

'Oh, shit!' Sally exclaimed. The blister in her mouth had burst and her tongue found the hanging skin, loose and irritating, adding to her growing frustration. She looked around at the office walls, seeking comfort from the photographic gallery of replica celebrities, but it didn't seem to help. Her voice became childlike as she protested, 'I can't see why they're so upset. The whole country's up in arms about their bonuses. Even the Chancellor, and he didn't exactly go to a local comprehensive school. And those city wankers – sorry, I mean bankers – don't strike anyone as shrinking violets. Surely they can take a little bit of verbal arse-kicking.'

'I think they're feeling sensitive from the recent bad press,' Lucy said. 'So you going to ring their PR people?'

Sally sighed heavily. 'Yes, but I'm in a meeting until lunchtime hah-hah. Then, after a glass or two of Chablis, I'll have the strength to deal with it.' She grinned at her assistant, and raised two fist-clenched arms. 'Then bring it on, baby!'

Lucy went and sat behind her own desk and exchanged a knowing smile with her employer. She knew how her boss would operate, starting with humble apologies before twisting it, so that the clients ended up feeling they were blame. In spite of knowing this, Lucy asked Sally what she intended saying to them.

'I shall of course apologise profusely.'

As Lucy guessed she would.

'Then I will point out in no uncertain terms how I told them right from the start that this particular Madonna does not sing. Not no way, not no how. Once this has been established and agreed, I will get them to admit that their smarmy slickers spiked our Madonna's drinks, and then when they humiliated her she quite naturally hit back at them. One poor female performer up against a whole roomful of baying hyenas? Enough to give her an inferiority complex, all those aggressive testosterone-fuelled males clubbing our poor baby seal.' She mimed violin playing. 'You wait: their PR department will end up apologising to me.'

'You think they'll use us again in the future?'

'Why wouldn't they? It'll be just another distant memory. A pissed Madonna replica's nothing compared to the bad press the banks are getting. Anyway, apart from this one little glitch on a Monday morning, it's not looking too bad the rest of the week. How's our Brad Pitt from Willesden Junction doing?'

'He tells me he's down to fourteen stone.'

'I suppose he's tall enough to get away with it. Only just though. But we can't take his word for it that he's lost two stone. Make an appointment for him to come in and see us and we'll check him out.'

The street door buzzer sounded. Sally frowned and looked at her watch. 'That can't be our new lookalike, can it? If it is, he's twenty-five minutes early.'

Lucy went into the small outer office, leaving the main office door open. The outer office was a small square room, doubling as a kitchen to brew tea and coffee, and a waiting room. Sally watched as Lucy pressed the talk button on the wall beside the entrance door.

'Star Repro. Who is it?'

A crackling voice announced he was Richard Deason. He apologised for being early and said he wouldn't mind waiting. Sally called to Lucy that they may as well see him now, and Lucy pressed the button to unlatch the street door, directing their appointment to the second floor. Lucy waited by the door while Sally pretended to busy herself looking through their latest client catalogue, and wondered who the visitor might look like. She had recently lost her Simon Cowell, who gave up his celebrity status reluctantly because he got more work and made more money as a central heating engineer. And she could do with another Mick Jagger, as their faux Rolling Stone had gone to that great celestial celebrity gig in the sky. So she hoped for one of those. But whoever this wannabe celebrity lookalike turned out to be, as long as it was instant recognition, they were in. Sometimes it required a little imagination and grooming to get them to a standard of instant recognition. But whoever she took on, even actor lookalikes like Bill Nighy or Timothy Spall, she had nothing to lose – in fact everything to gain – by expanding her list, because she could keep any amount of lookalikes on her books on the off-chance someone might want to hire anyone from a Nick Clegg lookalike to a Robbie Williams doppelganger or a Beyoncé Knowles imitator, and anyone she agreed to represent had to supply their own photographs, usually at a photographer of her recommendation, which meant she and Lucy received a bottle of expensive single malt at Christmas.

As the door of the outer office opened, she glanced up from her brochure and squinted. Lucy invited him in to the main office, and Sally caught a brief glimpse of her assistant walking behind the man as he entered, a puzzled expression on her face.

Sally's eyes swept over him, hoping that her first impression would bring an answer of some sort. The man was vaguely familiar, but she hadn't got a clue who he was supposed to represent. Usually their wannabe lookalikes made an effort and dressed the part, but this man...

She stood up, held out her hand, which he took in a rather limp, moist grip. He wore a dark grey suit, with small lighter grey checks, which was rather rumpled. He had a dark appearance, with a pugnacious face, and heavy chin with a five o'clock shadow.

She gestured for him to take a seat. Lucy sat behind her own desk, and Sally caught sight of her mouthing, 'Who is he?'

Sally ignored it, and concentrated on the wannabe client in front of her. Whoever he was supposed to resemble might be detectable but she had to admit she was at a loss. Was he a tennis player? Could be. Or maybe he was some obscure opera singer. She had a couple of those and they rarely worked. But she still took them on. You never know.

She switched on a disarming smile, false but striking, and said, 'Thank you for coming to see us, Richard. Good to meet you. But – and I'm going to hate myself for asking this, because I usually get the likenesses straightaway – but do you mind me asking whose public image you represent?'

Richard Deason grinned confidently, spread his arms and spoke in American accent marginally better than Dick Van Dyke's cockney. 'I think you might be too young to remember me, sweetheart, but how would it be if I gave you a big clue?'

American. That narrows the field, thought Sally. She shook her head. 'Yes, Richard, why don't you give me a clue?'

He thrust himself forward, elbows on knees, and gave her what he obviously thought was a sincere stare but verging on a leer. 'There can be no whitewash in the Whitehouse.' He sat back, pleased with himself, and waited for her response.

She raised her eyebrows. 'Rings a bell. Just can't quite... '

He chuckled. 'We share the same first name. But his nickname was Tricky Dickey.'

At last! Sally clicked her fingers. 'Of course! Richard Nixon.'

'The very same,' he grinned.

'Ah! We got there in the end.' Sally said with a breathy exhalation. 'We don't have any Richard Nixons.'

'So I would be unique in the field of lookalikes.'

'You would indeed, Richard. Just one thing though: we have loads of work for celebrity lookalike film stars, sports people, singers and models. But work for politician lookalikes tends to be thin on the ground.'

Performing his thrusting politician role, Deason aimed a finger at Sally. 'My time has come, Sally. Look at how many Nixons we've had in recent years. We had Anthony Hopkins in the title role, and more recently there was *Frost/Nixon.*' He pointed the finger at his own face. 'And these features look a lot more like Nixon than either Hopkins or Frank Langella.'

'Admittedly,' Sally agreed. 'But they were actors giving a terrific performance in major films.'

'Not all of them are famous actors,' he protested. 'What about that chap who got himself a job dancing with Meryl Streep in *The Iron Lady*? Just because he happened to look like Ronald Reagan.'

'Yes, but films like that tend to be few and far between. Our work tends to be weddings, functions, exhibitions and events. However, that said, you never know in this business. So I'm happy for Star Repro to represent you.'

Deason's mouth fell open, and there was a pause while he digested the good news, and then he looked as if he had won the lottery. 'Wow! That's fantastic. Absolutely fantastic.' He punched the air with his fist.

She raised a hand. 'But I don't want to raise your hopes. We may not find you anything. But you never know.'

She went on to spell out the terms and conditions of the agency, how he would have to agree to the signing of an exclusive contract which could be terminated by either party giving thirty days notice. Then she explained about the photographic session which was required as part of the conditions. Then Sally rose, shook hands with him, apologised for having to get on with her work, and sent him to sit with Lucy, who took down his contact details and told him there would be an agreement in the post that same day, with details of the photographer, who, following the session, would automatically forward the digital photos by email to Star Repro. A more than satisfied customer, Richard Deason departed and, apart from uploading his details on to their website, they thought that would be one of the last times they heard from him, unless someone was looking for a Richard Nixon, which was doubtful. But as Sally said: 'You never know. What have we got to lose?'

A week later, Richard Nixon was uploaded on to the Star Repro website. A day later the errant politician's lookalike phoned up to see if there had been any interest in booking him. At first, Sally was patient, and she and Lucy saw the funny side of it. But when he telephoned the next day, and the next, she gritted her teeth and asked him not to keep ringing, spelling out yet again the fact that not many wedding receptions or bar mitzvahs required dead American presidents and, it had to be said, there were not many fervent Nixon fans. Most of the calls were fielded by Lucy, and Sally was not so affected, although her irritation grew daily. And then, one late morning after Lucy had gone out to fetch them sandwiches for a working lunch, Sally took three phone calls and made three lucrative deals in only ten minutes, which was something of a record at their agency. The first was for a Ricky Gervais lookalike who wanted him to do the dance from *The Office* which, she assured the caller, would not be a problem. Neither would the request from her second caller who wanted a Gordon Ramsey capable of using bad language. Again, not a problem. Neither was the third call for a Johnny Depp in pirate costume. Sally was in a jubilant mood when the phone rang a fourth time. So when Richard Nixon, having ignored her request to stop pestering, rang to see if there had been anyone wanting to book Tricky Dickey yet, she was reasonably polite and talked to him patiently about leaving gaps of at least three months before contacting the agency. But their thick-skinned Nixon imitator, after being given the bum's rush, however civil it was on that occasion, went a stage further in his harassment. He took to bounding into their office, after he clearly waited in the street for the main door to the building to be opened by someone either entering or exiting. He thought he would amuse them by demonstrating his talent in his appalling American accent, and regaled them with Nixon speeches he had learnt, clearly hoping this gave him an advantage when it came to bookings. But no one wanted a Richard Nixon, as Sally screamingly pointed out the third time he gate-crashed their offices.

He was given thirty days termination of their contract. After that the building itself seemed to sigh with relief, things returned to normal, and he stopped calling. Pretty soon they forgot all about Richard Nixon, except when he became an amusing anecdote.

Six months later, just as they were about to leave the office for the evening, Sally was scouring the film trade papers, as she often did in case any lookalikes were needed as doubles or stand-ins in films, and what she saw made her eyes pop out on cartoon-stalks. They were making a film, a love story set at a USAF base in Mildenhall in1969, during Richard Nixon's informal visit to meet Harold Wilson. And the two politician's would be non-speaking roles but forming quite a background to the main story.

Sally could hardly believe it. A major film and a non-speaking Harold Wilson and a Richard Nixon were required. She didn't have a Harold Wilson on her books, but she knew where she could get her hands on a Richard Nixon. She quickly went through her computer database and called Richard Deason's number. It was answered after three rings.

'Hello. Is that you, Richard?' she said.

There was a slight chuckle at the other end. 'I thought I might hear from you, Sally.'

'Oh. Why's that?'

'The film with Richard Nixon in it.'

'Oh, you've heard about it.'

Another laugh. 'Not only have I heard about it, but I'm going to be in it.'

Sally imagined manic, taunting laughter in her head, and then heard herself swearing at the laughter as she wondered how Deason had managed to get cast. He probably knew nothing about doing deals, however, so she thought she would try to coax him into signing up to their agency again.

'Well, Richard,' she began, 'it's a pity we fell out, but even you have to admit you gave us a hard time, ringing up as you did every day, and then calling at the office unannounced. So let's forget the past, shall we, and I can offer you my services. If I say so myself, I'm very good at negotiating. So if you would like me to deal with the film company on your behalf, I'd be only too happy to help.'

'I'm sure you would. But you're too late, sweetheart. It's a done deal. And they're giving me two grand a day, with a guarantee of a week's work.'

Sally tried to swallow but her mouth felt dry. How on earth had he managed to pull off that amount for a non-speaking role?

'Well?' he said when she didn't reply. 'Not bad money for a walk-on, is it?'

'I must admit,' she said in a small, tremulous voice of defeat, 'it's a brilliant fee. How on earth did you manage it?'

He startled her by laughing loudly and she moved the receiver away from her ear.

'They don't call me Tricky Dickey for nothing,' he shouted.

He was still laughing loudly as she put down the receiver, telling herself that she would be working every day and earning good money, while Richard Nixon might have to wait another five or ten years until his services were required again. But she realised that was just sour grapes.

She looked at her watch. It was nearly time to go home. She waited for Lucy to return from the toilet and then suggested they go out to a wine bar for something to eat and drink. She couldn't wait to tell her assistant about Richard Nixon, and she had already made up her mind to deal with it positively. She could at least dine out on the story of Tricky Dickey's triumph.

A Brief History Of Soho

I was first attracted to visiting Soho along with some of my school friends in 1959 when I was only 16-years-old. The attraction was obvious to us young rites of passage teenagers. This was London's red-light district and trips out from the suburbs by underground train to this iniquitous district, just yards from the exit at Piccadilly Circus Tube station, was an audacious adventure. Prostitutes, in high heels, garish make-up and tight alluring dresses, still walked the streets plying their trade. Not that we could do anything but think wishfully at that age, but it was watching this daring and dangerous slice of immoral life, that was intoxicating to us libidinous, hormonal teenagers. When we got tired of merely watching the streetwalkers, we headed for the frothy coffee bars. Everyone had begun drinking proper coffee dispensed by Italian espresso machines. And skiffle, jazz and rock 'n' roll music venues sprang up, one of them being the 2i's coffee bar in Old Compton Street which gave early rock 'n' rollers a chance to show off their pop music abilities, and is known as the birthplace of British rock 'n' toll. This Soho culture was defined by the stage musical *Expresso Bongo*, a satire on the burgeoning rock 'n' roll industry. It starred Paul Scofield as a shady Tin Pan Alley manager, later made into a film starring Laurence Harvey in the same part, with Cliff Richard in the role of Bongo the singer, but the satire in the film was watered down.

The first coffee bar, Mika, opened in the early 1950s, which was later followed by hundreds of coffee bars, not only in Soho, but all over London. Some of them were gimmicky. I remember one in Richmond, Surry, called the Open City, where tables were set inside gondolas. But the trip to Soho to the Heaven and Hell Coffee Bar, was for us youngsters a treat like a child's visit to Disneyworld. We thought we were sophisticated sitting in a coffin in the darkened ambience of the establishment, done out like a Hammer horror film set sipping our foamy brew. But in that same year, the Street Offences Act, made it illegal for prostitutes to solicit for trade on the streets and they became call girls, euphemistically calling themselves 'models', in what might have been a pathetic attempt to fool the law but actually fooled no one. They advertised with notices stuck to seedy shop doorways or postcards distributed to telephone boxes where punters could find whatever was on offer, ring up, make an appointment and climb those rickety stairs to see if the 'model' looked anything like the photograph on the postcard. Sex shops increased during the sixties, as did clubs and restaurants, because Soho has for many years been London's adult playground, whether it be for sex, food and drink or music.

It was mainly food in the beginning. In the early days of the 16th century, when the area was under populated, it gained a reputation for its cuisine. The name Soho is believed to be the call of huntsmen, crying 'So-Hoe!' as they chased game in those fields and afterwards the dignitaries adjourned to a nearby banqueting house to feast on their catches. In the early 17th century a parish grew bit by bit north of Leicester Fields (later Leicester Square). In France the Huguenots were persecuted, and many escaped into exile and a life in London, gravitating towards the parish of Soho, opening French shops, cheap cafés and restaurants. Many other migrants were also attracted to the area, often exiled from far-flung European countries because of their religion or simply to search for a better life. Greek Street, at the heart of Soho, takes its name from the arrival of the many Greek Christians fleeing from persecution in the Ottoman Empire.

Music has always been a magnet to the area. In 1866 there were more than 30 music halls in the square mile, and in the 1930s American jazz was imported to Great Britain. Soho and West End clubs presented many famous American jazz musicians. In 1932 Louis Armstrong performed at Soho's most renowned theatre, The London Palladium in Argyll Street, at the north west of Soho, close to Oxford Circus. The Palladium, designed by the prominent theatre architect Frank Matcham, is a theatre that is loved by audiences and performers alike. It has hosted countless variety shows, pantomimes and musicals over the years, and was the venue for the long-running television show *Sunday Night at the London Palladium.*

Dozens of Soho theatres have disappeared since Victorian times, but there are still many in the area and on the fringes of the district. A popular theatre is the Piccadilly Theatre, situated as it is behind Piccadilly Circus's glittering array of neon. I remember in the seventies attending the first night of *Clarence Darrow for the Defence* with Henry Fonda in this one-man play giving a stunning performance. At the top end of Shaftsbury Avenue, facing Cambridge Circus is the Palace Theatre, home to *Les Miserables* for many years. I suppose it could be argued that most of the theatres in Shaftsbury Avenue are in Soho (their stage doors certainly lead into the district) and it has been asserted by many people that although Shaftsbury Avenue divides Soho and Chinatown, many people still regard that area immediately north of Leicester Square as Soho.

Another famous Soho theatre is the Prince Edward Theatre in Old Compton Street, a street which is now the heart of the gay community in Soho. The theatre was the first West End theatre to be built in 1930 and is named after Edward VIII, who abdicated and married Wallis Simpson. It became a cabaret restaurant in 1936, then after the war it was converted back to a theatre. In the past decades it has been the venue for many successful shows, including *Mama Mia* and *The Jersey Boys.* The return of *Miss Saigon* in May 2014 has broken all advance booking records with a staggering £4.4 million taken on the first day of sale.

One of the most famous theatres in the district, offering entertainment more in keeping with its dissolute image is the Windmill, in Great Windmill Street, which took its name from an actual windmill which stood there from the reign of Charles II until the late 18th century. The Windmill began life as the Palais de Luxe, showing silent films from 1909. Laura Henderson purchased it in 1930 and had it rebuilt as a small theatre and it reopened as the renamed Windmill Theatre in 1931. She is portrayed in a film about the Windmill starring Judi Dench, titled

Mrs Henderson Presents. After losses incurred presenting straight plays, new theatre Manager Vivian Van Damm persuaded the Lord Chamberlain (whose office controlled what was or wasn't allowed in theatres) that there is nothing obscene about the female form as nude statues are seen as works of art, and so the *tableaux vivants* was born in 1932. Young women could pose in the nude but had to remain absolutely still. During the war, and the heavy bombing of London during the Blitz, the Windmill's boast was that "We Never Closed". Following the sirens signalling an air raid the performers and crew would descend to deep basement shelter for safety, but after an air raid it was business as usual. In the late forties and early fifties, the Windmill became a training ground for many young comedians, who discovered it was hard getting laughs when all the mostly male audiences wanted was to ogle the immovable girls, perhaps hoping one might sneeze.

The man who found a way of circumventing the Lord Chamberlain's rules and presenting strip-tease was Paul Raymond, later known as the King of Soho when he became an immensely rich property tycoon, buying up leasehold and freehold buildings in the district. His Raymond Revuebar in Walker's Court just off Brewer Street, was a members only club, boasting a membership of thousands of eminent people from all walks of life. The neon sign outside his club gloated: "The World Centre of Erotic Entertainment". Raymond was portrayed in the 2013 film *The Look of Love* by Steve Coogan.

But Raymond was not the only Soho king. In St Anne's churchyard is the grave of Theodore I, King of Corsica. A German adventurer, Theodore made the acquaintance of Corsican rebels who sought freedom from Genoese rule and tyranny. Theodore

offered to take on the onerous task of organising an army and was duly elected King of Corsica. Eventually he made his way to England, attempting to raise support for his cause, but in 1749 he fell into debt and was jailed in a debtors' prison. He regained his freedom by declaring himself bankrupt but died in 1756. Horace Walpole was one of his supporters, and his epitaph, written by Walpole reads:

The grave, great teacher, to a level brings
Heroes and beggars, galley slaves and kings
But Theodore this moral learned ere dead
Fate poured its lessons on his living head
Bestowed a kingdom but denied him bread.

During the Blitz, St Anne's Church was bombed and burnt out on 24 September1940. The tower which to a certain extent survived was used as a chapel in the 1950s, partly restored in 1979 and the church was rebuilt in the early nineties. The tower is now a Grade II listed building.

In the sixties, satire and a strong urge to rock the establishment became all the rage, and a club was opened in Greek Street in 1961, aptly named the Establishment, founded by Peter Cook and Nicholas Luard. In the same year, not far from the Establishment, Private Eye, a satirical and current affairs magazine, began building its circulation. The magazine often exposed malpractices and regularly fought for survival when writs were issued against it. The Establishment shut its doors in 1964, while Private Eye continues to prosper.

As well as rock 'n' roll taking off in the fifties, it was jazz clubs that gripped Soho, the most renowned being Ronnie Scott's club. Scott was a saxophone player, and as well as playing with his own band, famous jazz musicians from all over the world enjoyed performing in the intimacy of his club. Another famous music venue was the Marquee Club, which moved from Oxford Street to Wardour Street in 1964. The Marquee began life as a jazz and skiffle club, but in the sixties became rhythm 'n' blues and rock, and musicians like the Yardbirds and Manfred Mann and the Rolling Stones often performed there in the early days.

Back in 1914 drinking laws became stringent and pubs were only allowed to open for so many hours in a day. Up until the early-eighties, the licensing laws continued to stop anyone enjoying an afternoon drink beyond 2.30 p.m., until pubs' early-doors when they opened again at 5.30 p.m. So to get around these severe drinking laws, Members Only drinking clubs opened up, many of them catering for misfits, artists, writers and actors. The most famous, or infamous of these, depending on your attitude, was the Colony Room, opened by Muriel Belcher in 1979 and regulars to the club included artists such as Lucian Freud, Francis Bacon, journalists Daniel Farson and Jeffrey Bernard, and many actors, writers and poets. It was rumoured that Dylan Thomas once puked on the carpet of the Colony Room.

The wonderful thing about Soho is that it still has the thrilling atmosphere of a sort of diverse enclave in the middle of London, an urban village teeming with creative characters. Media establishments, from recording studios and editing suites, to publishing houses are central to its existence And the small retail outlets are fascinating: off-licences which sell exotic liquor unobtainable in local supermarkets, including the mind-blowing absinthe; newsagents where you can purchase magazines and newspapers in hundreds of languages from all over the world; and music shops selling esoteric recordings of long-forgotten divas and crooners.

Soho has attracted and been home to hundreds of famous writers, politicians, artists and actors. Karl Marx who lived in the district for six years, held the second congress of the Communist League and wrote the Communist Manifesto in a room above the Red Lion pub in Great Windmill Street. The young nine-year-old Mozart stayed in Soho when he toured with his family, and a plaque commemorating his stay is fixed to the wall near the Stage Door of the Prince Edward Theatre. Other notable residents included Casanova, Canaletto, William Blake, Shelley and Isaac Newton, to name just a few The list goes on and on. For a complete record of Soho's famous residents and blue commemorative plaques, go to *www.thesohosociety.org.uk*

There have, of course, been many changes in the area over the years. The famous Windmill Theatre is now a table-dancing club rather than a cabaret venue, but I guess that's still in keeping with its reputation for titillation. And pubs like the Intrepid Fox in Wardour Street, where Mick Jagger famously persuaded Ronnie Wood to join the Rolling Stones, have long since disappeared. But changes happen in most districts. Thankfully Soho retains its cosmopolitan character, and long may that continue.

Some Famous Soho Pubs

French House

A favourite hang out for actors and artists. This Dean Street pub opened as the Wine House in 1910 by a German who was deported at the outbreak of war in 1914. The pub was bought by a Belgian who changed the name to the York Minster. His son, Gaston Berlemont was born on the premises in 1914, and ran the pub until his retirement in 1989. Although it was called the York Minster, it was known informally as 'The French' by its regular customers. After the fall of France during the second world war, General de Gaulle escaped to London and the French House became a regular meeting place for the Free French Forces. Anyone wanting a pint of beer in this pub will be disappointed, as traditionally they only serve beer in half pints. But this is one of Soho's favourite drinking dens, with a great tradition of hard-drinking writers and artists holding forth while inebriated, and one can imagine the mellifluous tones of Dylan Thomas in the late-forties and early-fifties rising above the then fug of a smoky atmosphere. He was probably inebriated when he left behind his only copy of *Under Milk Wood* there, which was later rescued by BBC producer Douglas Cleverdon. The bar is decorated with photographs of many well-known habitués from those halcyon days.

Coach and Horses

Just a stone's throw from 'The French', at the back of the Palace Theatre, this pub became famous in a Keith Waterhouse autobiographical play, *Jeffery Bernard is Unwell,* starring Peter O'Toole as Bernard. The play's setting is in the bar of the Coach and Horses, but the pub's landlord does not make an appearance, although Bernard is seen talking to him on the phone several times in the show. Norman Balen, landlord of the pub had a reputation for being the rudest pub landlord in London, an aspersion he never denied. The building itself is Grade II listed and dates from the 1850s. Journalists from Private Eye are regulars in the pub, as of course was Jeffrey Bernard, who wrote a regular column called "Low Life" for *The Spectator* magazine. Whenever Bernard missed a deadline from inebriation, the magazine would post a notice in its place saying: "Jeffrey Bernard is Unwell". He died from kidney failure in 1997.

Dog and Duck

Built in 1734 on the site of the Duke of Monmouth's home, on the corner of Bateman Street and Greek Street, the pub was rebuilt in 1897 and has remained largely unspoilt through the years. Even though it was redecorated in 2012, it still kept the dark oak wood and highly-glazed tiles which gives the pub its cosy atmosphere. Some of the famous regular customers were John Constable, Dante Gabriel Rossetti and George Orwell.

Red Lion

Not to be confused with the defunct pub of the same name in Great Windmill Street, this very traditional oak-panelled pub in Kingley Street has a great deal of atmosphere. The small bar at the front was used as a "jug and bottle", an area of a pub that sold booze to take home. Running parallel to Carnaby Street, this old Kingley Street pub is in close proximity to the London Palladium, and not far from where the Marquee Club was in the early sixties before it moved to Wardour Street. Many singers and performers popped in to the Red Lion for a pint or two, or Scotch and Coke which was a fashionable drink back then. I worked at the Red Lion for three months as a barman in 1966, and I can remember serving Eric Burden, lead singer of The Animals, with a pint.

Old Coffee House

Which is in fact a pub in Beak Street, just north of Golden Square. Back in the 18th century it was a coffee house, and a meeting house for political discussions, current affairs and debate. The décor has wonderful etched mirrors advertising ales from old non-existent breweries. But it also proudly displays a more modern history, a framed exhibit of David Beckham's signed photograph and a letter he wrote as a teenager explaining how he has received his first match fee and a bonus, and was now the proud possessor £250 in his bank

Shakespeare's Head

The pub is in Great Marlborough Street, which is a street Charles Darwin lived at for a year. Built in 1735, Shakespeare's Head was originally owned by Thomas and John Shakespeare, distant relatives of the great playwright. The pub's sign is a reproduction of the famous Martin Droeshout portrait, and on another part of the building is a life-size bust of Shakespeare, missing a hand which was lost during the First World War when a bomb dropped nearby.

Argyll Arms

Almost opposite the London Palladium, this is a pub that has been popular with theatregoers for years. An ornate late-Victorian pub, the interior has a fussy mahogany and etched glass enrichment typical of that era, providing plenty of genuine atmosphere.

De Hems

This old Dutch pub in Macclesfield Street is on the south side of Shaftsbury Avenue.

It has been a public house since 1688 when it was called the Horse and Dolphin. De Hem, a retired Dutch seaman, took it over in the early 20th century. He was obsessed with crustacean shells and decorated the bar with thousands of oyster shells, which were removed in the 1950s. During the Second World War Dutch resistance fighters gathered here.

Star and Garter

One of the earliest sites to be developed in Poland Street, the pub dates back to 1825, and is not far from where Percy Bysshe Shelley resided. A small wood-panelled traditional pub, there is plenty of history here in the framed prints and photographs and china jugs and porcelain. This is very much a small, cosy local, and has probably been like it for many years.

Pillars of Hercules

The pub dates back to 1733, but the present building was built around 1910. Charles Dickens referred to it in *A Tale of Two Cities*, and the street under the pub's arch is called Manette Street, named after Dr Manette in that novel. More recent literary figures who used the pub on a regular basis include Martin Amis, Ian McEwan, Julian Barnes and Clive James.

About The Author

David Barry has been an actor for almost 50 years having started as a child actor He played Frankie Abbott in the 70s sitcoms *Please, Sir!* and *Fenn Street Gang*, and also appeared in the film of *Please, Sir!* He has appeared in countless theatre and TV productions, including episodes of *The Bill*, *Never the Twain* and *A Mind to Kill*. His films include the Walt Disney version of *The Prince and the Pauper*, *Abandon Ship*, starring Tyrone Power and Mai Zetterling, and he played Elvis, Stratford Johns's nephew in *George and Mildred, the Movie*. His autobiography *Flashback – An Actor's Life* was published in 2006, and includes his childhood memoirs of touring Europe in *Titus Andronicus* in1957 with Laurence Olivier and Vivien Leigh as well as working on *Please, Sir!*. He has also recorded it as an audio book which is published by Oak Tree Press and is available on Amazon's Audible. His published novels include: *Mr Micawber Down Under*, (Hale Books) and three Inspector Lambert thrillers, *Each Man Kills*, *The Wrecking Bar* and *Missing Persons* written in his own name of Meurig Jones. *The Ice Cream Time Machine* (for children) *Willie the Actor*, *Careless Talk*, and *More Careless Talk* are all published by Andrews UK. His Freddie Weston thrillers include *Muscle* (Thames River Press) and *A Deadly Diversion* (Acorn Books). He lives in Tunbridge Wells and has two grown up children.

www.davidbarryauthor.co.uk
www.twitter.com/dbarrywriter
www.facebook.com/david.barry

Lightning Source UK Ltd.
Milton Keynes UK
UKHW041135170521
383863UK00003B/919

9 781783 338924